THE MOON TERROR

WILDSIDE PRESS

CONTENTS

The Moon Terror
By A. G. Birch

CHAPTER 1
THE DRUMS OF DOOM

THE first warning of the stupendous cataclysm that befell the earth in the third decade of the Twentieth Century was recorded simultaneously in several parts of America during a night in early June. But, so little was its awful significance suspected at the time, it passed almost without comment.

I am certain that I entertained no forebodings; neither did the man who was destined to play the leading role in the mighty drama that followed—Dr. Ferdinand Gresham, the eminent American astronomer. For we were on a hunting and fishing trip in Labrador at the time, and were not even aware of the strange occurrence.

Anyway, the nature of this first herald of disaster was not such as to cause alarm.

At twelve minutes past 3 o'clock a. m. during a lull in the night's aerial telegraph business, several of the larger wireless stations of the Western hemisphere simultaneously began picking up strange signals out of the ether. They were faint and ghostly, as if coming from a vast distance—equally far removed from New York and San Francisco, Juneau and Panama.

Exactly two minutes apart the calls were repeated, with clocklike regularity. But the code used—if it *were* a code—was undecipherable.

Until near dawn the signals continued—indistinct, unintelligible, insistent.

Every station capable of transmitting messages over such great distances emphatically denied sending them. And no amateur apparatus was powerful enough to be the cause. As far as any one could learn, the signals originated nowhere upon the earth. It was as if some phantom were whispering through the ether in the language of another planet.

Two nights later the calls were heard again, starting at almost the same instant when they had been distinguished on the first occasion. But this time they were precisely three minutes apart. And without the variation of a second they continued for more than an hour.

The next night they reappeared. And the next and the next. Now they began earlier than before—in fact, no one knew when they had started, for they were sounding when the night's business died down sufficiently for them to be heard. But each night, it was noticed, the interval between the signals was exactly one minute longer than the night before.

Occasionally the weird whispers ceased for a night or two, but always they resumed with the same insistence, although with a newly-timed interval.

This continued until early in July, when the pause between the calls had attained more than thirty minutes' duration.

Then the length of the lulls began to decrease erratically. One night the mysterious summons would be heard every nineteen and a quarter minutes; the next night, every ten and a half minutes; at other times, twelve and three-quarters minutes, or fourteen and a fifth or fifteen and a third.

Still the signals could not be deciphered, and their message—if they contained one—remained a mystery.

Newspapers and scientific journals at last began to speculate upon the matter, advancing all manner of theories to account for the disturbances.

The only one of these conjectures attracting widespread attention, however, was that presented by Professor Howard Whiteman, the famous director of the United States naval observatory at Washington, D. C.

Professor Whiteman voiced the opinion that the planet Mars was trying to establish communication with the earth—the mysterious calls being wireless signals sent across space by the inhabitants of our neighboring world.

Our globe, moving through space much faster than Mars, and in a smaller orbit, overtakes its neighboring planet once in a little over two years. For some months Mars had been approaching the earth. At the beginning of June it had been approximately 40,000,000 miles away, and at that time, Professor Whiteman pointed out, the strange wireless calls had commenced. As the two worlds drew closer together the signals increased slightly in power.

The scientist urged that while Mars remained close to us the government should appropriate funds to enlarge one of the principal wireless stations in an effort to answer the overtures of our neighbors in space.

But when, after two more days, the ethereal signals ceased abruptly and a week passed without their recurrence, Professor Whiteman's theory began to be derided, and the whole thing was dismissed as some temporary phenomenon of the atmosphere.

It was something of a shock, therefore, when, on the eighth night after the cessation of the disturbances, the calls were suddenly resumed—much louder than before, as if the power creating their electrical impulses had been increased. Now wireless stations all over the world plainly heard the staccato, mystifying challenge coming out of the ether.

This time, too, the interval between the signals was of a new length—eleven minutes and six seconds.

The next day the matter took on still further importance.

Scientists all along the Pacific Coast of the United States reported that in the night their seismographs had recorded a series of light earthquakes; and it was noted that these tremors had occurred precisely eleven minutes and six seconds apart—simultaneously with the sounding of the mysterious wireless calls!

After that the aerial signals did not stop during any part of the twenty-four hours. And the earth shocks continued, gradually increasing in severity. They kept perfect time with the signals through the ether—a shock for every whisper, a rest for every pause. In the course of a couple of weeks the quakes attained such force that in many places they could be distinctly felt by anyone standing still upon solid ground.

Science now became fully aware of the existence of some new and sinister—or at least unfathomed—force in the world, and began to give the matter profound study.

However, both Dr. Ferdinand Gresham and I remained in complete ignorance of these events; for, as I have said, we were in the interior of Labrador. We both possessed a keen love of the wilderness, where, in vigorous sports, we renewed our energy for the work to be done in the cities—the doctor's as director of the great astronomical observatory at the National University; mine in the prosaic channels of business.

To the public, which knew him only through his books and lectures, Dr. Gresham perhaps appeared the last person in the world anyone would seek for a companion: a man silent, preoccupied, austere, unsociable. But underneath this aloofness and taciturnity was a character of rare strength, good nature and lovableness. And, once beyond the barriers of civilization, his austerity vanished, and he became a prince of good fellows, actually reveling in hardships and danger.

The complete change in him on such occasions brought to mind a strange phase of his life about which not even I, his most intimate associate, knew anything—a period in which he had undertaken a mysterious pilgrimage alone into the dark interior of China.

I only knew that fifteen years before he had gone in quest of certain amazing astronomical discoveries rumored to have been made by Buddhist savants dwelling in monasteries far back in the Himalayas or the Tian-Shan, or some of those inaccessible mountain fastnesses of Central Asia. After more than four years he had dragged back, ill and suffering, bearing hideous disfigurations upon his body, the look in his eyes of a man who had seen hell, and maintaining inviolate silence regarding his experiences.

On regaining his health after the Chinese adventure, he had immersed himself in silence and work, and year by year since then I had seen him steadily rise in prominence in his profession. Indeed, his name had come to stand for vastly more in the scientific world than merely the advancement of astronomical knowledge. He was a deep student along many lines of scientific endeavor—electricity, chemistry, mathematics, physics, geology, even biology. To the development of wireless telegraphy and the wireless transmission of electrical energy he had devoted particular effort.

The doctor and I had left New York a few days before the wireless disturbances began. Returning by a small private vessel, which was not equipped with wireless, we continued in ignorance of the world's danger.

It was during our homeward sea voyage that

the earthquakes began to grow serious. Many buildings were damaged. In the western portions of the United States and Canada a number of persons were killed by the collapse of houses.

Gradually the affected area expanded. New York and Nagasaki, Buenos Aires and Berlin, Vienna and Valparaiso began to take their places on the casualty list. Even modern skyscrapers suffered broken windows and falling plaster; sometimes they shook so violently that their occupants fled to the streets in a panic. Water and gas mains began to break.

Before long, in New York, one of the railroad tunnels under the Hudson River cracked and flooded, causing no loss of life, but spreading such alarm that all the tubes under and out of Manhattan were abandoned. This brought about a fearful congestion of traffic in the metropolis.

Finally, toward the beginning of August, the earthquakes became so serious that the newspapers were filled every day with accounts of the loss of scores—sometimes hundreds—of lives all over the world.

Then came a happening fraught with a monstrous new terror, which was revealed to the public one morning just as day dawned in New York.

During the preceding night, a great Atlantic liner, steaming westward approximately along the fiftieth parallel of latitude, had *run aground* about 700 miles east of Cape Race, Newfoundland—at a point where all nautical charts showed the ocean to be *nearly two miles deep!*

Within an hour there had come reports of a similar nature from other ships two or three hundred miles distant from the first one. There was no telling how vast in extent might be the upheaved portion of the sea bottom.

Hardly had the wireless stations finished taking these startling stories from midocean before there began to arrive equally strange reports from other quarters of the globe.

Someone discovered that the sea level had risen almost six feet at New York. The Sahara Desert had sunk to an unknown depth, and the sea was rushing in, ripping vast channels through the heart of Morocco, Tripoli and Egypt, obliterating cities and completely changing the face of the earth.

Within a few hours the high waters in New York harbor receded about a foot. Mount Chimborazo, the majestic peak of more than 20,000 feet altitude in the Ecuadorean Andes, began to fall down and spread out over the surrounding country. Then the mountains bordering the Panama Canal started to collapse for many miles, completely blocking that famous waterway.

In Europe the Danube River ceased to flow in its accustomed direction and began, near its junction with the Save, to pour its waters back past Budapest and Vienna, turning the plains of western Austria into a series of spreading lakes.

The world awoke that summer morning to face a more desperate situation than ever had confronted mankind during all the centuries of recorded history.

And still no plausible explanation of the trouble—except the Martian theory of Professor Howard Whiteman—was forthcoming.

Men were dazed, astounded. A feeling of dread and terror began to settle upon the public.

At this juncture, realizing the need of some sort of action, the President of the United States urged all the other civilized nations to send representatives to an international scientific congress in Washington, which should endeavor to determine the origin of the terrestrial disturbances and, if possible, suggest relief.

As speedily as airplanes could bring them, an imposing assemblage of the world's leading scientists gathered in Washington.

Because of his international reputation and the fact that the congress held its sessions at the United States naval observatory, of which he was chief, Professor Whiteman was chosen president of the body.

For a week the scientists debated—while the world waited in intense and growing anxiety. But the learned men accomplished nothing. They could not even agree. The battle seemed one of man against nature, and man was helpless.

In a gloomy state of mind they began to consider adjournment. At 10 o'clock on the nineteenth of August the question of terminating the sessions was scheduled for a final vote.

That night, as the hands of the clock on the wall above the presiding officer's head drew near the fateful hour, the tension throughout the assemblage became intensely dramatic.

Even, after the sound of the clock's striking had died out upon the stillness of the room, Professor Whiteman remained seated; he seemed haggard and downcast. At last, however, he drew himself up and opened his lips to speak.

At that moment a secretary tiptoed swiftly in and whispered briefly to the presiding officer. Professor Whiteman gave a start and answered something that sent the secretary hurrying out.

Betraying strange emotion, the scientist now addressed the assemblage. His words came haltingly, as if he feared they would be greeted with ridicule.

"Gentlemen," he said, "a strange thing has happened. A few minutes ago—the wireless signals that have always accompanied the earthquakes ceased abruptly. In their place came— a mysterious summons out of the ether— whence no one knows—demanding a conversation with the presiding officer of this body. The sender of the message declares his communication has to do with the problem we have been trying to solve. Of course—this is probably some hoax—but our operator is greatly excited over the circumstances surrounding the call, and urges that we come to the wireless room at once!"

Leading the way to another part of the observatory grounds, Professor Whiteman ushered the company into the operating room of the wireless plant—one of the most powerful in the world.

A little knot of observatory officials already was clustered about the operator, their manner denoting that something unusual had been going on.

At a word from Professor Whiteman, the operator threw over his rheostat and the hum of the rotary spark filled the room. Then his fingers played on the key while he sent out a few signals.

"I'm letting them—*him*—know you're ready, sir," the operator explained to the astronomer, in a tone filled with awe.

A few moments slipped by. Everyone waited breathlessly, all eyes glued upon the apparatus, as if to read the momentous message that was expected to come from—no one knew where.

Suddenly there was an involuntary movement of the muscles of the operator's face, as if he were straining to hear something very faint and far away; then he began writing slowly upon a pad that lay on his desk. At his elbow the scientists unceremoniously crowded each other in their eagerness to read: "To the Presiding Officer of the International Scientific Congress, Washington," he wrote. "I am the dictator of human destiny. Through control of the earth's internal forces I am master of every existing thing. I can blot out all life—destroy the globe itself. It is my intention to abolish all present governments and make myself emperor of the earth. As proof of my power to do this, I"—there was a pause of several seconds, which seemed like hours in the awful stillness—"I shall, at midnight tomorrow, Thursday (Washington time), cause the earthquakes to cease until further notice.

"KWO."

CHAPTER 2
THE DICTATOR OF DESTINY

By THE next morning the entire civilized world knew of the strange and threatening communication from the self-styled "dictator of human destiny."

The members of the scientific congress had sought to keep the matter secret, but all the larger wireless stations of North America had picked up the message, and thence it found its way into the newspapers.

Ordinarily, such a communication would have attracted nothing more than laughter, as a harmless prank; but the increasing menace of the earthquakes had wrought a state of nervous tension that was ready to clothe the whole affair with sinister significance.

It was an alarmed and hysterical public that gathered in the streets of all the great cities soon after daylight. One question was on every tongue:

Who was this mysterious "KWO," and was his message actually a momentous declaration to the human race, or merely a hoax perpetrated by some person with an over-vivid imagination?

Even the signature to the communication was such as to arouse curiosity. Was it a name? Or a combination of initials? Or a title, like

"Rex," signifying king? Or a nom de plume?
Or the name of a place? No one could say.

Any one capable of discovering the secrets of
the earth's internal forces, and harnessing those
forces for his own ends, unquestionably was
the most wonderful scientist the world had
ever seen; but, though every important nation
of the globe was represented at the scientific
congress in Washington, not one of those
representatives had ever heard of successful
experiments along this line, or knew any prominent scientist named KWO, or one possessing
initials that would make up that word. The
name sounded Oriental, but certainly no country of the Orient had produced a scientist of
sufficient genius to accomplish this miracle.

It was a problem concerning which the best-
informed persons knew no more than the most
untutored child, but one which was of para-
mount importance to the group of savants
assembled in Washington. Until more light
could be shed on this subject they were power-
less to form any conclusions. Accordingly,
their first effort was to get into further communication with their unknown correspondent.

All through the night the operator at the
naval observatory's wireless plant in Washington sat at his key, calling over and over again
the three letters that constituted mankind's
only knowledge of its adversary:

"KWO—KWO—KWO!"

But there was no answer. Absolute silence
enveloped the menacing power. "KWO" had
spoken. He would not speak again. And

after twelve hours even the most persistent members of the scientific body—who had remained constantly in the wireless room throughout the night—reluctantly desisted from further attempts at communication.

Even this failure found its way into the newspapers and helped to divide public opinion. Many persons and influential papers insisted that "KWO's" threat was nothing more than a hoax. Others, however, were inclined to accept the message as the serious declaration of a human being with practically supernatural powers. In advancing this opinion they were supported by the undeniable fact that from the time the mysterious "KWO" began his efforts to communicate with the head of the scientific congress, until his message had been completed, the strange wireless signals accompanying the earth tremors had ceased entirely—a thing that had not happened before. When he was through speaking, the signals had resumed their clocklike recurrence. It was as if some power had deliberately cleared the ether for the transmission of this proclamation of mankind.

A feeling of dread—of monstrous uncertainty—hung over everyone and increased as the day wore on. Ordinary affairs were neglected, while the crowds in public places steadily increased.

By nightfall of Thursday even the loudest scoffers at the genuineness of the "dictator's" threat began to display symptoms of the general uneasiness.

Would the earthquakes begin to subside at midnight?

Upon the answer to this question hung the fate of the world.

It was an exceedingly hot night in most parts of the United States. Scarcely anywhere was a breath of air stirring; the whole country was blanketed by a suffocating wave of humidity. Low clouds that presaged rain—but never brought it—added to the general feeling of apprehension. It was as if all nature had conspired to furnish a dramatic setting for the events about to be enacted.

As midnight drew near the excitement became intense. In Europe, as well as in America, vast throngs filled the streets in front of the newspaper offices, watching the bulletin boards. The Consolidated News Syndicate had arranged special radio service from various scientific institutions—notably the Washington naval observatory, where savants were watching the delicate instruments for recording earth shocks —and any variation or subsidence in the tremors would be flashed to newspapers everywhere.

When the hands of the clocks reached a point equivalent to two minutes of midnight, Washington time, a vast hush fell upon the assembled thousands. The very atmosphere became aquiver with suspense.

But if the scene in the streets was exciting, that within the instrument room of the United States naval observatory, where the members of the international scientific congress waited, was dramatic beyond description.

About the room sat the scientists and a couple of representatives from the Consolidated

News. Professor Whiteman himself was stationed at the seismographs, while at his elbow sat Professor James Frisby, in direct telephone communication with the wireless operator in another part of the grounds.

The light was shaded and dim. The heat was stifling. Not a word was spoken. Scarcely a muscle moved. All were painfully alert.

Every eleven minutes and six seconds the building was shaken by a subterranean shock. The windows rattled. The floor creaked. Even the chairs seemed to lift and heave. It had been that way for weeks. But would this night see the end?

With maddening slowness, the hands of the clock on the wall—its face illuminated by a tiny electric lamp—drew toward 12 o'clock.

Suddenly there came one of the earthquakes, that, while no different from its predecessors, heightened the tension like the crack of a whip.

All eyes flew to the timepiece. It registered thirty-four seconds past 11:49 o'clock.

Therefore, the next tremor would occur at precisely forty seconds after midnight.

If the unknown "KWO" were an actual being, and kept his word—at that time the shocks would begin to subside!

The suspense became terrible. The faces of the scientists were drawn and pale. Beads of perspiration stood out on every brow. The minutes passed.

The electric correcting-device on the clock gave a sharp *click*, denoting midnight. Forty seconds more! The suffocating atmosphere

seemed almost to turn cold under the pressure
of anxiety.

Then, almost before any one could realize it,
the earthquake had come and gone! And not
one particle of diminution in its violence had
been felt!

A sigh of relief involuntarily passed around
the room. Few moved or spoke, but there was
a lessening of the strain on many faces. It
was too soon yet, of course, to be sure, but—
in most hearts there began to dawn a faint ray
of hope that, after all, this "dictator of human
destiny" might be a myth.

But suddenly Professor Frisby raised his
hand to command quiet, and bent more intently
over his telephone.

A short silence followed. Then he turned
to the gentlemen and announced in a voice
that seemed curiously dry:

"The operator reports that no wireless signal
accompanied this last earthquake."

Again the nerve tension in the assembly
leaped like an electric spark. Several more
minutes passed; then came another quake.

All eyes sped to Professor Whiteman but he
remained absorbed at his seismographs.

In this silence and keen suspense eleven
minutes and six seconds again dragged by.
Another earthquake came and went. Once
more Professor Frisby announced that there
had been no wireless signal attending the
tremor. The savants began to settle themselves
for a further wait, when——

Professor Whiteman left his instrument and

came slowly forward. In the dim light his face looked lined and gray.

"Gentlemen," he said, *"the earthquakes are beginning to subside!"*

For a moment the scientists sat as if stunned. Every one was too appalled to speak or move. Then the tension was broken by the rush of the Consolidated News men from the room to get their momentous tidings out to the world.

After that the ground shocks died out with increasing rapidity. In an hour they had ceased entirely, and the tortured planet once more was still.

But the tumult among the people had only started!

With a sudden shock the globe's inhabitants realized that they were in the grip of an unknown being endowed with supernatural power. Whether he were man or demigod, sane or mad, well-disposed or malignant—no one could guess. Where was his dwelling-place, whence the source of his power, what would be the first manifestation of his authority, or how far would he seek to enforce his control? Only time could answer.

As this situation dawned upon men, their fears burst all bounds. Frantic excitement took possession of the throngs.

Only at the naval observatory in Washington was there calmness and restraint. The gathering of scientists spent the night in earnest deliberation of the course to be followed.

Finally it was decided that nothing should be done for the present; they would merely await events. When it had suited the mysteri-

ous "KWO" to announce himself to the world
he had done so.   Thereafter, communication
with him had been impossible.   Doubtless when
he was ready to speak again he would break
his silence—not before.   It was reasonable to
suppose that, now he had proved his power,
he would not be long in stating his wishes or
commands.

Events soon showed this surmise was correct.

Promptly at noon the next day—there having
in the meantime been no recurrence of the
earthquakes or electrical disturbances of the
ether—the wireless at the naval observatory
again received the mysterious call for the presiding officer of the scientific congress.

Professor Whiteman had remained at the
observatory, in anticipation of such a summons,
and soon he, with other leading members of the
scientific assembly, was at the side of the operator in the wireless room.

Almost immediately after the call:

"KWO—KWO—KWO!"

went forth into the ether, there came a response
and the operator started writing:

"To the Presiding Officer of the International
Scientific Congress:

"Communicate this to the various governments of the earth:

"As a preliminary to the establishment of
my sole rule throughout the world, the following demands must be complied with:

"First: All standing armies shall be dis-
banded, and every implement of warfare, of
whatsoever nature, destroyed.

"Second: All war vessels shall be assembled —those of the Atlantic fleets midway between New York and Gibraltar, those of the Pacific fleets midway between San Francisco and Honolulu—and sunk.

"Third: One-half of all the monetary gold supply of the world shall be collected and turned over to my agents at places to be announced later.

"Fourth: At noon on the third day after the foregoing demands have been complied with, all the existing governments shall resign and surrender their powers to my agents, who will be on hand to receive them.

"In my next communication I will fix the date for the fulfillment of these demands.

"The alternative is the destruction of the globe.　　　　　　　　　　　　"KWO."

It was on the evening of this eventful day that Dr. Gresham and I returned from Labrador. A little after 10 o'clock we landed in New York and, taking a taxicab at the pier, started for our bachelor quarters in apartments near each other west of Central Park.

As we reached the center of town we were amazed at the excited crowds that filled the streets and at the prodigious din raised by newsboys selling extras.

We stopped the car and bought papers. Huge black headings told the story at a glance. Also, at the bottom of the first page, we found a brief chronological summary of all that had happened, from the very beginning of the mysterious wireless signals three months before. We scanned it eagerly.

When I finished the newspaper article I turned to my companion—and was struck with horror at the change in his appearance!

He was crumpled down upon the seat of the taxi, and his face had taken on a ghastly hue. Only his eyes held a sign of life, and they seemed fixed on something far away—something too terrifying to be a part of the world around us.

His lips moved, and presently he murmured, as if talking in his sleep:

"It has come! The Seuen-H'sin—*the terrible Seuen-H'sin!*"

An instant later, with a great effort, he drew himself together and spoke sharply to the chauffeur:

"Quick! Never mind those addresses we gave you! Rush us to the Grand Central Station! *Hurry!*"

As the car suddenly swerved into a side street, I turned to the doctor.

"What's the matter? Where are you going?" I asked.

"To Washington!" he snapped in reply. "As fast as we can get there!"

"In connection with this earthquake terror?"

"Yes!" he told me; "for——"

There was a pause, and then he finished in a strange, awed voice:

"What the world has seen of this devil 'KWO' is only the faintest prelude to what may come—events so terrible, so utterly opposed to all human experience, that they would stagger the imagination! *This is the beginning of the dissolution of our planet!*"

CHAPTER 3
THE SORCERERS OF CHINA

"DOUBTLESS you never heard of the Seuen-H'sin."

The speaker was Dr. Ferdinand Gresham, and these were the first words he had uttered since we had entered our private compartment on the midnight express for Washington, an hour before.

I lowered my cigar expectantly.

"No," I said; "never until you spoke the name in a momentary fit of illness this evening."

The doctor gave me a swift, searching glance, as if questioning what I might have learned. Presently he went to the door and looked out into the passage, apparently assuring himself no one was within hearing; then, locking the portal, he returned to his seat and said:

"So you never heard of the Seuen-H'sin—'The Sect of the Two Moons'? Then I will tell you: the Seuen-H'sin are the sorcerers of China, and the most murderously diabolical breed of human beings on this earth! They are the makers of these earthquakes that are aimed to wreck our world!"

The astronomer's declaration so dumbfounded me that I could only stare at him, wondering if he were serious.

"The Seuen-H'sin are sorcerers," he repeated presently, "whose devilish power is shaking our planet to the core. And I say to you solemnly that this 'KWO'—who is Kwo-Sung-tao, high priest of the Seuen-H'sin—is a thousand times more dangerous than all the conquerors in history! Already he has absolute control of a hundred millions of people—mind and body, body and soul!—holding them enthralled by black arts so terrible that the civilized mind can not conceive of them!"

Dr. Gresham leaned forward, his eyes shining brightly, his voice betraying deep emotion.

"Have you any idea," he demanded "what goes on in the farthermost interior of China? Has *any* American or European?

"We read of a republic superseding her ancient monarchy, and we meet her students who are sent here to our schools. We hear of the expansion of our commerce along the jagged edges of that great Unknown, and we learn of Chinese railroad projects fostered by our financiers. But no human being in the outside world could possibly conceive what takes place in that gigantic shadowland—vague and vast as the midnight heavens—a continent unknown, impenetrable!

"Shut away in that remote interior—in a valley so little heard of that it is almost mythical —beyond trackless deserts and the loftiest mountains on the globe—this terrible sect of sorcerers has been growing in power for thousands of years, storing up secret energy that some day should inundate the world with horrors such as never have been known!

"And yet you never heard of the Seuen-H'sin! No; nor has any other Caucasian, except, perhaps, a chance missionary or two.

"But I tell you *I have seen them!*"

Dr. Gresham was becoming strangely excited, and his voice rose almost shrilly above the roar of the train.

"I have seen them," he went on. "I have crossed the Mountains of Fear, whose summits tower as high as from the earth to the moon, and I have watched the stars dance at night upon their glaciers. I have starved upon the dead plains of Dzun-Sz'chuen, and I have swum the River of Death. I have slept in the Caves of Nganhwiu, where the hot winds never cease and the dead light their campfires on their journey to Nirvana. And I have seen, too"—there was a strange, entranced look on his face as he spoke—"I have seen the Shadow of God on Tseih Hwan and K'eech-ch'a-gan! But in the end I have dwelt in Wu-yang!

"Wu-yang," he continued, after a brief pause, "is the center of the Seuen-H'sin—a wondrous dream city beside a lake whose waters are as opalescent as the sky at dawn; where the gardens are sweet-scented with a million blooms, and the air is filled with bird songs and the music of golden bells.

"But forgive me," sighed the doctor, rousing himself from his ecstatic train of thought; "I speak in the allegories of another land!"

We were silent for a time, until finally I suggested:

"And the Seuen-H'sin—The Sect of the Two Moons?"

"Ah, yes," responded Dr. Gresham. "In Wu-yang the Beautiful I dwelt among them. For three years that city was my home. I labored in its workshops, studied in its schools, and—yes; I will admit it—I took part in those hellish ceremonies in the Temple of the Moon God—to save myself from death by fiendish torture. And, as my reward, I watched those devils at their miraculous business—*the making of another moon!*"

We smoked a moment in silence. Then:

"Surely," I objected, "you do not believe in miracles!"

"Miracles? Yes," he affirmed seriously— "miracles of science. For the sorcerers of China are scientists—the greatest that this world has yet produced. Talk to me of modern progress—our arts and sciences, our discoveries and inventions! Bah! They are child's play —clap-trap!—beside the accomplishments of this race of Chinese devils! We Americans boast of our Thomas Edison. Why, the Seuen-H'sin have a thousand Edisons!

"Think of it—thousands of years before Copernicus discovered that the earth revolves around the sun, Chinese astronomers understood the nature of our solar system and accurately computed the movements of the stars. The use of the magnetic compass was ancient even in those days. A thousand years before Columbus was born their navigators visited the western coast of North America and maintained colonies for a time. In the year 2657 B. C. savants of the Seuen-H'sin completed engineering projects on the Yellow River that never have been surpassed. And forty centuries before Christ the physicians of China practised inoculation against smallpox and wrote erudite books on human anatomy.

"Scientists? Why, man alive, the Seuen-H'sin are the greatest scientists that ever lived! But they haven't the machinery or the materials or the factories that have made the Western nations great. There they are—shut up in their hidden valley, with no commercial incentives, no contact with the world, no desire but to study and experiment.

"Their scientific development through centuries beyond number has had only one object, which was the basis of their fanatical religion —the discovery of a means to split this earth and project an offshoot into space to form a second moon. And if our train stopped this minute you probably could feel them somewhere beneath you—hammering—hammering —hammering away at the world with their terrible and mysterious power, which even now it may be too late to stop!"

The astronomer rose and paced the length of the compartment, apparently so deep in thought that I was loth to disturb him. But finally I asked:

"Why do these sorcerers desire a second moon?"

Dr. Gresham resumed his seat and, lighting a fresh cigar, began:

"Numerous legends that are almost as old as the human race represent that the earth once had two moons. And not a few modern astronomers have held the same theory. Mars has two satellites, Uranus four, Jupiter five and Saturn ten. The supposition of these scientists is that the second satellite of the earth was shattered, and that its fragments are the meteors which occasionally encounter our world in their flight.

"Now, in the far, far distant past, before the days of Huang-ti and Yu—even before the time of the great semi-mythical kings, Yao and Shun—there ruled in China an emperor of peculiar fame—Ssu-chuan, the Universal.

"Ssu-chuan was a man of weak character and mediocre talents, but his reign was the greatest in all Chinese history, because of the intelligence and energy of his empress, Chwang-Keang.

"In those days, the legends tell us, the world possessed two moons.

"At the height of his prosperity Ssu-chuan fell in love with a very beautiful girl, called Mei-hsi, who became his mistress.

"The Empress Chwang-Keang was as plain as Mei-hsi was beautiful, and in time the mistress prevailed upon her lord to plot his wife's murder, so that Mei-hsi might be queen. Chwang-Keang was stabbed to death one evening in her garden.

"With her death begins the history of Seuen-H'sin.

"Simultaneous with the murder of the empress, one of the moons vanished from the sky. The Chinese legends say the spirit of the great ruler took refuge upon the satellite, which fled with her from sight of the earth. Modern

astronomers say the satellite probably was
shattered by an internal explosion.

"Now that the firm hand of Chwang-Keang
was lifted from affairs of state, everything went
wrong in China—until the country reverted
virtually to savagery.

"At last Ssu-chuan aroused himself from
his pleasures sufficiently to take alarm.   He
consulted his priests and seers, who assured him
that heaven was angry because of the murder
of Chwang-Keang. Never again, they said,
would China know happiness or prosperity
until the vanished moon returned, bringing the
spirit of the dead empress to watch over the
affairs of her beloved land. Upon her return,
however, the glory of China would rise again,
and the Son of Heaven would rule the world.

"Upon receiving these tidings, the legends
relate, Ssu-chuan was consumed with pious
zeal.

"Upon a lofty mountain behind the city he
built the most magnificent temple in the world,
and installed there a special priesthood to
beseech heaven to restore the second moon.
This priesthood was named the Seuen-H'sin,
or Sect of the Two Moons. The worship of
the Moon God was declared the state religion.

"Gradually the belief that the Seuen-H'sin
was to restore the second moon—and that,
when this happened, the Celestial Kingdom
again would enjoy universal rule—became the
fanatical faith of a fourth of China.

"But finally, in a fit of remorse, Ssu-chuan
burnt himself alive in his palace.

"The empire of Ssu-chuan dissolved, but the

Seuen-H'sin grew greater. Its high priest attained the most terrible and far-reaching power in China. But in the second century B. C., Shi-Hwang-ti the great military emperor made war upon the sorcerers and drove them across the Kuen-lum mountains. Still they retained great wealth and power; and in Wu-yang they made a city that is the dream spot of the world, equipped with splendid colleges for the study of astronomy and the sciences and magic.

"As astronomical knowledge increased among the Seuen-H'sin, they came to believe that the moon once was a part of the earth, having been blown out of the hollow now filled by the Pacific Ocean. In this theory certain eminent American and French astronomers lately have concurred.

"The Chinese sorcerers conceived the idea that by scientific means the earth again could be rent asunder, and its offshoot projected into space to form a second moon. Henceforth, all their labors were directed toward finding that means. And the lust for world domination became the religion of their race.

"When I dwelt among them they seemed to be drawing near their goal—and now they probably have reached it!

"But if we may judge from these demands of Kwo-Sung-tao, their plans for world conquest have taken a new and simpler turn: by threatening to use their mysterious force to dismember the globe they hope to subjugate mankind just as effectively as they expected to do by creating a second moon and fulfilling their prophecy.   Why wreck the earth, if they can conquer it by threats?

"If they are able to enforce their demands it will not be long before civilization is face to face with those powers of evil that grind a quarter of China's millions beneath their ghastly rule — a rule of fanaticism and terror that would stun the world!"

Dr. Gresham paused and peered out the window.   There was an unearthly look on his face when he again turned toward me.

"I have seen," he said, "those hideous powers of the Seuen-H'sin—things of horror such as the Western mind can not conceive!   When the beating of my heart shall cease forever, when my body has been buried in the grave, and when the Seuen-H'sin torture scars"— he tore open his shirt and revealed frightful cicatrices upon his chest—"have vanished in the final dissolution, then, even then, I shall not forget those devils out of hell in Wu-yang, and I shall feel their power clutching at my soul!"

CHAPTER 4
DR. GRESHAM TAKES COMMAND

IT WAS shortly before dawn when we alighted from the train in Washington. Newsboys were calling extras:

"Terrible disaster! Nine thousand lives lost in Mississippi River!"

Purchasing copies of the papers, Dr. Gresham called a taxicab and directed the chauffeur to take us as rapidly as possible to the United States naval observatory in Georgetown. We read the news as we rode along.

The great railroad bridge across the Mississippi River at St. Louis had collapsed, plunging three trains into the stream and drowning virtually all the passengers; and a few minutes later the Mississippi had ceased to flow past the city, pouring into a huge gap that suddenly had opened in the earth at a point about twenty-five miles northwest of the town.

Nearly everyone in St. Louis who could get an automobile had started for the point where the Mississippi was tumbling into the earth, and before long a vast crowd had assembled along the edges of the steaming chasm, watching the phenomenon.

Suddenly there had come a heavy shock underground and the crack had heaved nearly shut, sending a vast geyser, the full width of

' the stream, spouting a couple of thousand feet aloft. A few moments later this huge column of water had thundered back upon the river banks where the spectators were gathered, stunning and engulfing thousands. At the same time the gash had opened again and into it the torrent had swept the helpless multitude. Then it had closed once more and remained so, and the river had resumed its flow.

It was estimated that more than 9,000 persons had perished.

"Kwo-Sung-tao has stopped his earthquakes," remarked Dr. Gresham, when he had finished scanning the newspaper reports, "but irreparable damage has been done. Enough water doubtless has found its way into the heated interior of the globe to form a steam pressure that will play havoc."

Soon we drew up at the white-domed observatory crowning the wooded hill beyond Wisconsin Avenue. It was our good fortune to find Professor Howard Whiteman and several prominent members of the international scientific congress still there.

After a brief conversation with these gentlemen—to whom he was well known by reputation—Dr. Gresham drew Professor Whiteman and two of his chief assistants aside and began questioning them about the disturbances. He gave not the slightest hint of his knowledge of the Seuen-H'sin.

The doctor was particularly interested in every detail regarding the course taken by the quakes—whether or not all of them had come from the same direction, what that direction was, and how far away the point of origin seemed to be.

Professor Whiteman said the seismographs indicated the tremors all had come from one direction—a point somewhere to the northwest —and had traveled in a general southeasterly course. It was his opinion that the seat of the disturbances was about 3,000 miles distant— certainly not more than 4,000 miles.

This appeared greatly to surprise my companion and to upset whatever theories he might have in mind. Finally he asked to see all the data on the tremors, especially the actual seismograph records. At once we were taken to the building where these records were kept.

For more than an hour Dr. Gresham intently studied the charts and calculations, making new computations of his own and referring to numerous maps. But the longer he worked, the more puzzled he became.

Suddenly he looked up with an exclamation, and after seemingly weighing some new idea, he turned to me and said:

"Arthur, I need your help. Go to one of the newspaper offices and look through the files of old copies for an account of the capture of the Pacific steamship *Nippon* by Chinese pirates. Try to find out what cargo the vessel carried. If the newspaper accounts do not give this, then try at the State Department. But hurry!"

We had kept our taxicab waiting, so I was soon speeding toward one of the newspaper offices on Pennsylvania Avenue. As I rode along, I brought to mind the strange and terrible story of the great Pacific liner.

The *Nippon* was the newest and largest of
the fleet of huge ships in service between San
Francisco and the Orient. Fifteen months
previous, while running from Nagasaki to
Shanghai, across the entrance to the Yellow
Sea, she had encountered a typhoon of such
violence that one of her propeller shafts was
damaged, and after the storm abated she was
obliged to stop at sea for repairs.

It was an intensely dark, quiet night. About
midnight the officer of the watch suddenly
heard from the deck amidship a wild, long-
drawn yell. Then all became quiet again. As
he started to descend from the bridge he heard
bare feet pattering along the deck below. And
then more cries arose forward—the most awful
sounds. Rushing to his cabin, he seized a
revolver and returned to the deck.

Surging over the rail at a dozen points were
savage, half-naked yellow forms, gripping long,
curved knives—the dreaded but almost-extinct
Chinese pirates of the Yellow Sea. The fiends
swiftly attacked a number of passengers who
had been promenading about, murdering them
in cold blood.

Meanwhile, other pirates were rushing to all
parts of the ship.

As soon as he recovered from his first horri-
fied shock, the officer leaped toward a group
of the Chinamen and emptied his revolver into
them. But the pirates far outnumbered the
cartridges in his weapon, and when his last
bullet had been fired several of the yellow devils
darted at him with gleaming knives. Where-

upon the officer turned and fled to the wireless operator's room near by.

He got inside and fastened the heavy door just a second ahead of his pursuers. While the Chinamen were battering at the portal, he had the operator send out wireless calls for help, telling what was occurring on board.

Several ships and land stations picked up the strange story as far as I have related it, at which point the message ceased abruptly.

From that instant the *Nippon* vanished as completely as if she never had existed. Not one word ever again was heard of the vessel or of a single soul on board.

It required only a few minutes' search through the newspaper files to find the information I sought, and soon I was back at the observatory.

Dr. Gresham greeted me eagerly.

"The steamship *Nippon*," I reported, "carried a cargo of American shoes, plows and lumber."

My friend's face fell with keen disappointment.

"What else?" he inquired. "Weren't there other things?"

"Lots of odds and ends," I replied—"pianos, automobiles, sewing machines, machinery—"

"*Machinery?*" the doctor shot out quickly. "What kind of machinery?"

I drew from my pocket the penciled notes I had made at the newspaper office and glanced over the items.

"Some electrical equipment," I answered. "Dynamos, turbines, switchboards, copper cable

—all such things—for a hydro-electric plant near Hongkong."

"Ah!" exclaimed the doctor in elation. "I was sure of it! We may be getting at the mystery at last!"

Seizing the memoranda, he ran his eyes hurriedly down the list of items. Profound confidence marked his bearing when he turned to Professor Whiteman a moment later and said:

"I must obtain an immediate audience with the President of the United States. You know him personally. Can you arrange it?"

Professor Whiteman could not conceal his surprise.

"Concerning these earthquakes?" he inquired.

"Yes!" my friend assured him.

The astronomer looked at his colleague keenly.

"I will see what I can do," he said. And he went off to a telephone.

In five minutes he was back.

"The President and his cabinet meet at 9 o'clock," announced the director. "You will be received at that hour."

Dr. Gresham looked at his watch. It was 8:30.

"If you will be so kind," said Dr. Gresham, "I would like to have you go with us to the President—and Sir William Belford, Monsieur Linné and the Duke de Rizzio as well, if they are still here. What we have to discuss is of the utmost importance to their governments, as well as to ours."

Professor Whiteman signified his own willingness to go, and went to hunt the other gentlemen.

This trio my friend had named comprised undoubtedly the leading minds of the international scientific congress. Sir William Belford was the great English physicist, head of the British delegation to the congress. Monsieur Camille Linné was the leader of the French group of scientists, a distinguished electrical expert. And the Duke de Rizzio was the famous Italian inventor and wireless telegraph authority, who headed the representatives from Rome.

The director soon returned with the three visitors, and we all hastened to the White House. Promptly at 9 o'clock we were ushered into the room where the nation's chief executive and his cabinet—all grim and careworn from a night of sleepless anxiety—were in session.

As briefly as possible, Dr. Gresham told the story of the Seuen-H'sin.

"It is their purpose," he concluded, "to crack open the earth's crust by these repeated shocks, so that the water from the oceans will pour into the globe's interior. There, coming into contact with incandescent matter, steam will be generated until there is an explosion that will split the planet in two."

It is hardly to the discredit of the President and his advisers that they could not at once accept so fantastic a tale.

"How can these Chinamen produce an artificial quaking of the earth?" asked the President.

"That," replied the astronomer frankly, "I

am not prepared to answer yet—although I have a strong suspicion of the method employed."

For the greater part of an hour the gentlemen questioned the astronomer. They did not express doubt of his veracity in his account of the Seuen-H'sin, but merely questioned his judgment in attributing to that sect the terrible power to control the internal forces of the earth.

"You are asking us," objected the Secretary of State, "virtually to return to the Dark Ages and believe in magicians and sorcerers and supernatural events!"

"Not at all!" returned the astronomer. "I am asking you to deal with modern facts—to grapple with scientific ideas that are so far ahead of our times the world is not prepared to accept them!"

"Then you believe that an unheard-of group of Chinamen, hiding in some remote corner of the globe, has developed a higher form of science than the brightest minds of all the civilized nations?" remarked the Attorney General.

"Events of the last few weeks seem to have demonstrated that," replied Dr. Gresham.

"But," protested the President, "if these Mongolians aim at splitting the globe to project a new moon into the sky, why should they be satisfied with an entirely different object—the acquisition of temporal power?"

"Because," the scientist informed him, "the acquisition of temporal power is their ultimate goal. Their only object in creating a second moon is to fulfill the prophecy that they should rule the earth again when two moons hung in the sky. If they can grasp universal rule *without* splitting the globe—merely by *threatening* to do so—they are very much the gainers."

The Secretary of the Navy next voiced a doubt.

"But it is evident," he remarked, "that if Kwo-Sung-tao makes the heavens fall, they will fall on his own head also!"

"Quite true," admitted the astronomer.

"Then," persisted the Secretary, "is it likely that human beings would plot the destruction of the earth when they know it would involve them, too, in the ruin?"

"You forget," returned the doctor, "that we are dealing with a band of religious fanatics— undoubtedly the most irrational zealots that ever lived!

"Besides," he added, "the Seuen-H'sin, in spite of its threats, does not expect to destroy the world completely. It contemplates no more than the blowing of a fragment off into space."

"What, then, shall be done?" inquired the President.

"Place at my disposal one of the fastest destroyers of the Pacific fleet—equipped with certain scientific apparatus I shall devise—and let me deal with the Seuen-H'sin in my own way," announced the astronomer.

The gathering at once voiced vigorous objection.

"What you propose might mean war with China!" exclaimed the President.

"Not at all," was the answer. "It is possible not a single shot will be fired. And, in any event, we will not go anywhere near China."

The consternation of the officials increased.

"We shall not go near China," Dr. Gresham explained, "because I am certain the leaders of the Seuen-H'sin are no longer there. At this very hour, I am convinced, Kwo-Sung-tao and his devilish band are very much nearer to us than you dream!"

The gathering broke into excited discussion.

"After all," remarked Sir William Belford, "suppose this expedition *should* plunge us into hostilities. Unless something is done quickly, we are likely to meet a fate far worse than war!"

"I am willing to do anything necessary to remove this menace from the world—if the menace actually exists," the President stated. "But I am unable to convince myself that these wireless messages threatening mankind are not merely the emanations of a crank, who is taking advantage of conditions over which he has no control."

"But I maintain," argued Sir William, "that the sender of these messages *has* fully demonstrated his control over our planet. He prophesied a definite performance, and that prophecy was fulfilled to the letter. We can not attribute its fulfillment to natural causes, nor to any human agency other than his. I say it is time we recognized his power, and dealt with him as best we may."

Several others now began to incline to this view.

Whereupon the Attorney General joined in the discussion with considerable warmth.

"I must protest," he interposed, "against what seems to me an extraordinary credulity upon the part of many of you gentlemen. I view this affair as a rational human being. Some natural phenomenon occurred to disturb the solidity of the earth's crust. That disturbance has ceased. Some joker or lunatic was lucky enough to strike it right with his prediction of this cessation—nothing more. The disturbance may never reappear. Or it may resume at any moment and end in a calamity, no one can foretell. But when you ask me to believe that these earthquakes were due to some human agency—that a mysterious bugaboo was responsible for them—I tell you *no!*"

Monsieur Linné had risen and was walking nervously up and down the room. Presently he turned to the Attorney General and remarked:

"That is merely your opinion, sir. It is not proof. Why may these earthquakes not be due to some human agency? Have we not begun to solve all the mysteries of nature? A few years ago it was inconceivable that electricity could ever be used for power, heat and light. May not many of the inconceivable things of today be the commonplace realities of tomorrow? We have earthquakes. Is it beyond imagination that the forces which produce them can be controlled?"

"Still," returned the Attorney General vigorously, "my answer is that we have no adequate reason for attributing either the appearance or the cessation of these earthquakes to any human power! And I am unalterably opposed to making the government of the United States ridiculous by fitting out a naval expedition to combat a phantom adversary."

Dr. Gresham now had risen and was standing behind his chair, his face flushed and his eyes shining. At this point he broke sharply into the discussion, the cold, cutting force of his words leaving no doubt of his decision.

"Gentlemen," he said, " I did not come here to *argue*; I came to *help*! As surely as I am standing here, our world is upon the brink of dissolution! And I alone may be able to save it! But, if I am to do so, you must agree absolutely to the course of action I propose!"

He glanced at his watch. It was 10 o'clock.

"At noon," he announced, in tones of finality, "I shall return for my answer!"

And he turned and started for the door.

In the tenseness of those last few moments, almost no one had been conscious of the soft buzzing of the President's telephone signal, or of the fact that the executive had removed the receiver and was listening into the instrument.

Now, as Dr. Gresham reached the door, the President lifted a hand in a commanding gesture and cried: "Wait!"

The astronomer turned back into the room.

For a minute, perhaps, the President listened at the telephone; and as he did so the expression of his face underwent a grave change. Then, telling the person at the other end of the wire to wait, he addressed the gathering:

"The naval observatory at Georgetown is on the 'phone. There has just been another communication from 'KWO.' It says——"

The executive again spoke into the telephone: "Read the message once more, please!"

After a few seconds, speaking slowly, he repeated:

" 'To the Presiding Officer of the International Scientific Congress:

" 'I hereby set the hour of noon, on the twenty-fifth day of the next month, September, as the time when I shall require compliance with the first three demands of my last communication. The fulfillment of the fourth demand—the resignation of all the existing governments—therefore, will take place on the twenty-eighth day of September.

" 'In order to facilitate the execution of my plans, I shall require an answer by midnight next Saturday, one week from today, from the governments of the world as to whether they will comply with my terms of surrender. In the absence of a favorable reply by that time, I shall terminate, absolutely and forever, all negotiations with the human race, and shall cause the earthquakes to resume and continue with increasing violence until the earth is shattered.   " 'KWO.' "

When the President finished reading and hung up the telephone, a deathlike silence fell upon the gathering. Dr. Gresham, standing by the door, made no further movement to depart.

The President glanced at the faces about him, as if seeking some solution of the problem. But no aid was forthcoming from that source.

Suddenly the silence was broken by a chair being pushed back from the table, and Sir William Belford rose to speak.

"Gentlemen," he said, "this is no time for hesitation. If the United States does not immediately grant Dr. Gresham's request for a naval expedition against the Seuen-H'sin, Great Britain *will* do so!"

At once Monsieur Linné spoke up: "And that is the attitude of France!"

The Duke de Rizzio nodded, as if in acquiescence.

Without further hesitation, the President announced his decision.

"I will take the responsibility for acting first and explaining to Congress afterward," he said. And, turning to the Secretary of the Navy, he added:

"Please see that Dr. Gresham gets whatever ships, men, money and supplies he needs—without delay!"

CHAPTER 5
BEGINNING A STRANGE VOYAGE

TELEGRAPHIC orders flew thick and fast from Washington, and before nightfall two high naval officers left the capital for San Francisco to expedite arrangements for the expedition.

Meanwhile, the doctor hurried me back to New York with instructions to visit the electrical concern that had manufactured the dynamos and other equipment that had been aboard the steamship *Nippon,* and obtain all the information possible about this machinery. This I did without difficulty.

The government arranged with a big electrical machinery firm to place a section of its plant at Dr. Gresham's disposal, and as soon as the astronomer returned to New York he plunged into feverish activity at this shop, personally superintending the construction of his paraphernalia.

As fast as this apparatus was completed it was rushed off by airplane to the Mare Island navy yard near San Francisco.

It had already been settled that I was to accompany the doctor on his expedition, so my friend availed himself of my services for many tasks. Some of these struck me as most odd.

I had to purchase a large quantity of fine silks of brilliant hues, mostly orange, blue and violet; also a supply of grease paints and other materials for theatrical make-up. These articles were sent to Mare Island with the scientific equipment.

Day by day, the week which "KWO" had granted the world to announce its surrender slipped by. During this period the utmost secrecy was maintained regarding the projected naval expedition. The public knew nothing of the strange story of the sorcerers of China. Anxiety was universal and acute.

Many persons favored surrender to the would-be "emperor of the earth," arguing that any person who proposed to abolish war possessed a greatness of spirit far beyond any known statesman; they were willing to entrust the future of the world to such a dictator. Others contended that the demand for destruction of all implements of war was merely a precautionary measure against resistance to tyranny.

Dr. Gresham urged to the authorities at Washington that in dealing with so unscrupulous and inhuman a foe as the sorcerers, equally unscrupulous methods were justified. He proposed that the nations inform "KWO" they would surrender, to ward off the immediate resumption of the earthquakes and give the naval expedition time to accomplish its work.

But the governments could not agree upon any course of action; and in this indecision the last day of grace drew toward its close.

As midnight approached, vast crowds assembled about the newspaper offices, eager to learn what was going to happen.

At last the fateful hour came—and passed in silence. The world had failed to concede its surrender.

Five minutes more slipped into eternity.

Then there was a sudden stir as bulletins appeared. Their message was brief. At three minutes past 12 o'clock the wireless at the United States Naval Observatory had received this communication:

"To All Mankind:

"I have given the world an opportunity to continue in peace and prosperity. My offer has been rejected. The responsibility is upon your own heads. This is my final message to the human race.   "KWO."

Within an hour the earthquakes resumed. And they were repeated, as before, exactly eleven minutes and six seconds apart.

With their reappearance vanished the last vestige of doubt that the terrestrial disturbances were due to human agency—to a being powerful enough to do what he chose with the planet.

By the end of three days it was noticed that the shocks were increasing in violence much more swiftly than previously, as if the earth's crust had been so weakened that it could no longer resist the hammering.

At this juncture Dr. Gresham announced that he was ready to leave for the Pacific Coast.

The government had one of its giant mail planes waiting at an aviation field on Long Island, and in its comfortable enclosed interior we were whisked across the continent.

In less than two days we alighted at the Mare Island Navy Yard, where the *Albatross,* the destroyer that was to serve for our expedition, lay at our disposal.

The *Albatross* was the newest, largest and fastest destroyer of the Pacific fleet—an oil-burning craft carrying a crew of 117 men.

Most of the boxes and crates of material that we had sent from New York being already on deck, the astronomer immediately went to work with a corps of the navy's electricians to assemble his apparatus.

I was sent off to find six men tailors all familiar with the making of theatrical costumes, who were willing to undertake a mysterious and dangerous sea voyage; also two actors skilled in make-up.

All during this time the earthquakes never varied from their intervals of eleven minutes and six seconds, and the seriousness of affairs throughout the world continued to grow. In Europe and America deep fissures, sometimes hundreds of miles long, now appeared in the ground. Gradually it became apparent that these cracks in the earth's crust were confined within a definite area, which roughly formed a circle touching the Mississippi River on the west and Serbia on the east.

Then, on the morning after our arrival in San Francisco, half a dozen noted scientists—

none of whom, however, belonged to the little group that had been taken into Dr. Gresham's confidence regarding the Seuen-H'sin—issued a warning to the public.

They prophesied that the world soon would be rent by an explosion, and that the portion within the circular area already outlined would be blown away into space or would be pulverized.

Nearly one-fifth of the entire surface of the earth was included in this doomed circle, embracing the most civilized countries of the globe—the eastern half of the United States and Canada; all of the British Isles, France, Spain, Italy, Portugal, Switzerland, Belgium, Holland and Denmark; and most of Germany, Austria-Hungary and Brazil. Here, too, were located the world's greatest cities—New York, London, Paris, Berlin, Vienna, Rome, Chicago, Boston, Washington and Philadelphia.

The scientists urged the people of the eastern United States and Canada to flee immediately beyond the Rocky Mountains, while the inhabitants of western Europe were advised to take refuge east of the Carpathians.

The first result of this warning was simply to daze the public. But in a few hours the true character of the predicted happenings dawned upon people in full force. Then terror —blind, sickening, unreasoning terror—seized the masses, and there began the most gigantic and terrible exodus in the history of the earth —a migration that in a few hours developed into a mad race of half the planet's inhabitants across thousands of miles.

Transportation systems were seized by the frenzied throngs and rendered useless in the jam. People started frantically in airplanes, automobiles, horsedrawn vehicles — even on foot. All restraints of law and order vanished in the hideous struggle of "every man for himself."

At last, toward midnight of this day, Dr. Gresham finished his work. Together we made a final tour of inspection through the ship.

Electrical equipment was scattered everywhere—several big generators, a whole battery of huge induction coils, submarine telephones, switchboards with strange clocklike devices mounted upon them, and reels of heavy copper wire.

One thing that particularly attracted my attention was an instrument at the very bottom of the ship's hold. It looked like the seismographs used on land for recording earthquakes. I observed, too, that the wireless telegraph equipment of the destroyer had been much enlarged, giving it a wide radius.

At the finish of our inspection, the doctor sought Commander Mitchell, the vessel's chief officer, and announced:

"You may start at once—on the course I have outlined."

A few minutes later we were silently speeding toward the Golden Gate.

Dr. Gresham and I then went to bed.

When we awoke the next morning we were out of sight of land and were steaming at full speed north in the Pacific Ocean.

CHAPTER 6
THE COASTS OF MYSTERY

HOUR after hour the destroyer kept up her furious pace almost due north in the Pacific. We never came in sight of land, and it was impossible for me to guess whither we were bound.

Throughout the first day Dr. Gresham remained in his stateroom—silent, troubled, buried in a mass of arithmetical calculations.

In another part of the ship the six tailors I had brought on board labored diligently upon a number of Chinese costumes, the designs for which the doctor had sketched for them.

And on deck a detail of men was busy unpacking and assembling one of the two hydroplanes that had been taken on board.

By the middle of the second day Dr. Gresham laid aside his calculations and began to display the keenest interest in the details of the voyage. About midnight he had the ship stopped, although neither land nor any other craft was in sight; whereupon he went to the hold and studied the hydro-seismographs. To my surprise I saw that, although we were adrift upon the restless ocean, the instrument was recording tremors similar to earthquakes on land. These occurred precisely eleven minutes and six seconds apart.

Seeing my astonishment, the doctor explained:

"It is possible to record earth shocks even at sea. The ocean bed imparts the jar to the water, through which the tremor continues like the wave caused by throwing a stone into a pond."

But the thing which seemed to interest my friend most was that these shocks now appeared to be originating at some point to the northeast of us, instead of to the northwest, as we had noted them in Washington.

Soon he ordered the vessel started again, this time on a northeasterly course, and the next morning we were close to land.

Dr. Gresham, who at last had begun to throw off his taciturn mood, told me this was the coast of the almost unsettled province of Cassiar, in British Columbia. Later, as we began to pass behind some rugged islands, he said we were entering Fitzhugh Sound, a part of the inland passage to Alaska. We were now approximately 300 miles northwest of the city of Vancouver.

"Somewhere, not far to the north of here," added the doctor, "is 'The Country of the Great Han,' where Chinese navigators, directed by Huei-Sen, a Buddhist priest, landed and founded colonies in the year 499 A. D. You will find it all recorded in 'The Book of Changes,' which was written in the reign of Tai-ming, in the dynasty of Yung: how, between the years 499 and 556, Chinese adventurers made many trips across the Pacific to these colonies, bringing to the wild inhabitants the laws of Buddha, his sacred books and images; building stone temples; and causing at last the rudeness of the natives' customs to disappear."

With this my friend left me, upon some summons from the ship's commander, and I could learn no more.

The region into which we were now penetrating was one of the wildest and loneliest on the North American continent. The whole coastline was fringed by a chain of islands—the tops of a submerged mountain range. Between these islands and the continent extended a maze of deep, narrow channels, some of which connected in a continuous inland waterway. The mainland was a wilderness of lofty peaks, penetrated at intervals by tortuous fiords, which, according to the charts, sometimes extended erratically inland for a hundred miles or more. Back from the coast a few miles, we could see the elevated gorges of the main range filled with glaciers, and occasionally one of these gigantic rivers of ice pushed out to the Sound, where its face broke away in an endless flotilla of icebergs.

The only dwellers in this region were the few inhabitants of the tiny Indian fishing villages, scattered many miles apart; and even of these we saw not a sign throughout the day.

Toward nightfall the doctor had the *Albatross* drop anchor in a quiet lagoon, and the hydroplane that had been assembled on deck was lowered to the water.

It now lacked two nights of the period of full moon, and the nearly round satellite hung well overhead as darkness fell, furnishing, in that clear atmosphere, a beautiful illumination in which every detail of the surrounding mountains stood forth.

As soon as the last trace of daylight had vanished, Dr. Gresham, equipped with a pair of powerful binoculars, appeared on deck, accompanied by an aviator. He said nothing about where he was going; and, knowing his moods so intimately, I realized it was useless to seek information until he volunteered it. But he handed me a large sealed envelope, remarking:

"I am going for a trip that may take all night. In case I should not return by sun-up you will know something has happened to me, and you are to open this envelope and have Commander Mitchell act upon the instructions it contains."

With this, he gave me a firm handclasp that plainly was meant for a possible farewell, and followed the aviator into the plane. In a few moments they were off, their new type of noiseless motor making scarcely a sound, and soon were climbing toward the summits of the snow-covered peaks to the eastward. Almost before we realized it they were lost from sight.

It was my intention to keep watch through the night for the return of my friend; but after several hours I fell asleep and knew no more until dawn was reddening the mountaintops. Then the throbbing of the destroyer's engines awakened me, and I hurried on deck to find Dr. Gresham himself giving orders for the vessel's movements.

The scientist never once referred to the events of the night as he partook of a light breakfast and went to bed. However, I could tell by his manner that he had not met with success.

Slowly the ship continued northward most of that day, through the awesome fastnesses of Fitzhugh Sound, until we reached the mouth of a grim fiord set down on the charts as Dean Channel. Here we cast anchor.

Late in the afternoon Dr. Gresham put in his appearance, viewed the mainland through his glasses, and then went into the ship's hold to study his earthquake recorder. What he observed apparently pleased him.

This night also was moonlit and crystal-clear; and, as before, when daylight had departed, the doctor reminded me of the sealed orders I held against his failure to return at sunrise, bade me farewell, and started off in the airship, flying straight toward the range of peaks that walled the eastern world.

On this occasion a series of remarkable happenings removed all difficulty of my keeping awake.

About 10 o'clock, when I chanced to be visiting in the commander's cabin, an officer came and informed us of some strange lights that had been observed above the mountains at a distance inland. We went on deck and beheld a peculiar and inexplicable phenomenon.

To the northeast the heavens were illuminated at intervals by flashes of white light, extending, fan-shaped, far overhead. The display was as brilliant and beautiful as it was mysterious. For a good while we watched it—until I was suddenly struck with the regularity of the intervals between the flashes. Timing the lights with my watch, I found they occurred *precisely eleven minutes and six seconds apart!*

With a new idea in mind, I made a note of the exact instant when each flash appeared; then I went down into the hold of the ship and looked at Dr. Gresham's hydro-seismograph. As I suspected, the aerial flashes had occurred simultaneously with the earthquakes.

When I returned to the deck the phenomenon in the sky had ceased.

But shortly after midnight another portentous event occurred to claim undivided attention.

The powerful wireless of the *Albatross,* which could hear messages coming and going throughout the United States and Canada, as well as over a great part of the Pacific Ocean, began to pick up accounts of terrible happenings all over the world. The fissures in the ground, which had appeared shortly before we left San Francisco, had suddenly widened and lengthened into a nearly unbroken ring about the portion of the globe from which the inhabitants had been warned to flee. Within this danger-circle the ground had begun to vibrate heavily and continuously—as the lid to a tea-kettle dances when the pressure of steam beneath it is seeking a vent.

The flight of the public from the doomed area had grown into an appalling hegira—until a fresh disaster, a few hours ago, had suddenly cut it short: the Rocky Mountains had begun to fall down throughout most of their extent, obliterating all the railroads and other highways that penetrated their chain. Now the way to safety beyond the mountain was hopelessly blocked.

And with this catastrophe hell had broken loose among the people of America!

It was near dawn before these stories ceased. The officers and I were still discussing them when day broke and we beheld Dr. Gresham's hydroplane circling high overhead, seeking a landing. In a few minutes the doctor was with us.

The instant I set eyes on him I knew he had met with some degree of success. But he said nothing until we were alone and I had poured out the tale of the night's happenings.

"So you saw the flashes?" he remarked.

"We were greatly puzzled by them," I admitted. "And you?"

"I was directly above them and saw them made," he announced.

"Saw them *made*?" I repeated.

"Yes," he assured me; "indeed, I have had a most interesting trip. I would have taken you with me, only it would have increased the danger, without serving any purpose. However, I am going on another jaunt tonight, in which you might care to join me."

I told him I was most eager to do so.

"Very well," he approved; "then you had better go to bed and get all the rest you can, for our adventure will not be child's play."

The doctor then sought the ship's commander and asked him to proceed very slowly up the deep and winding Dean Channel, keeping a sharp ·lookout ahead. As soon as the vessel started we went to bed.

It was mid-afternoon when we awakened. Looking out our cabin portholes, we saw we were moving slowly past lofty granite precipices that were so close it seemed we might almost reach out and touch them. Quickly we got on deck.

Upon being informed that we had gone about seventy-five miles up Dean Channel, Dr. Gresham stationed himself on the bridge with a pair of powerful glasses, and for several hours gave the closest scrutiny ahead, as new vistas of the tortuous waterway unfolded.

We now seemed to be passing directly into the heart of the lofty Cascade Mountain range that runs the length of Cassiar Province in British Columbia. At times the cliffs bordering the fiord drew in so close that it seemed we had reached the end of the channel, and again they rounded out into graceful slopes thickly carpeted with pines. Still there was no sign that the foot of man ever had trod this wilderness.

Late in the afternoon Dr. Gresham became very nervous, and toward twilight he had the ship stopped and a launch lowered.

"We will start at once," he told me, "and Commander Mitchell will go with us."

Taking from me the sealed letter of instructions he had left in my care before starting on his airplane trips the previous nights, he handed it to the commander, saying: "Give this to the officer you leave in charge of the ship. It is his orders in case anything should happen to us and we do not return by morning. Also, please triple the strength of the night watch. Run your vessel close under the shadows of the bank, and keep her pitch-dark. We are now in the heart of the enemy's country, and we can't tell what sort of a lookout he may be keeping."

While Commander Mitchell was attending to these orders, the doctor sent me below to get a pair of revolvers for each of us. When I returned, the three of us entered the launch and put off up the channel.

Slowly and noiselessly we moved ahead in the gathering shadows near shore. The astronomer sat in the bow, silent and alert, gazing constantly ahead through his glasses.

We had proceeded scarcely fifteen minutes when the doctor suddenly ordered the launch stopped. Handing his binoculars to me and pointing ahead beyond a sharp bend we were just rounding, he exclaimed excitedly: *"Look!"*

I did so, and to my astonishment saw a great steamship lying at a wharf!

Commander Mitchell now had brought his glasses into use, and a moment later he leaped to his feet, exclaiming:

"My God, men! *That's the vanished Pacific liner Nippon!*"

An instant more and I also had discerned the name, standing out in white letters against the black stern. Soon I made a second discovery that thrilled me with amazement: faint columns of smoke were rising from the vessel's funnels, as if she were manned by a crew and ready to sail!

"Let us get back to the *Albatross*," said Dr. Gresham, "as quickly as we can!"

On board the destroyer, we hastened to our cabin, where Chinese suits of gorgeous silk had been laid out for us; they were part of the quantity of such garments my six tailors had been making. There were two outfits for each—one of flaming orange, which we put on first, and one of dark blue, which we slipped on over the other. Then one of the actors was summoned, and he made up our faces so skillfully that it would have been difficult to distinguish us from Chinamen.

When the actor had left the room, the doctor handed me the revolvers I had carried before, and also a long, villainous-looking knife. To these he added a pair of field glasses. After similarly arming himself, he announced:

"I feel I must warn you, Arthur, that this trip may be the most perilous of your whole life. All the chances are against our living to see tomorrow's sun, and if we die it is likely to be by the most fiendish torture ever devised by human beings! Think well before you start!"

I promptly assured him I was willing to go wherever he might lead.

"But where," I asked, "is that to be?"

"We are going," he answered, "into the hell-pits of the Seuen-H'sin!"

And with that we entered the launch and put off into the coming darkness.

CHAPTER 7
THE MOON GOD'S TEMPLE

It was not long before the launch again brought us within sight of the mystery ship, the *Nippon*.

Near it we landed and had the seaman take the launch back to the destroyer. With a final inspection of our revolvers and knives, we started forward through the rocks and timber toward the vessel.

It was the night of the full moon, but the satellite had not yet risen above the mountains to the east, so we had only the soft gleam of the stars to light us on our way. In spite of the northern latitude, it was not uncomfortably cold, and soon we were spellbound by the gorgeous panorama of the night. Above us, through the lattice-work of boughs, the calm, cold stars moved majestically across the black immensity of space. The dark was fragrant with the scent of pines. Strangely hushed and still the universe appeared, as if in the silence world were whispering to world.

We could now feel the periodic earthquakes very plainly—as if we were directly over the seat of the disturbances.

In a few minutes we reached the edge of the clearing about the *Nippon's* wharf. There were no buildings, so we had an unobstructed view of the vessel, lying tied to the dock. Two or three lights shone faintly from her portholes, but no one was visible about her.

The wharf was at the entrance to a little side valley that ran off to the southwest through a break in the precipitous wall of the fiord. From this ravine poured a turbulent mountain stream which, I recalled from the ship's charts, was named Dean River.

After a brief look around we discovered a wide, smooth roadway leading from the wharf into the valley, paralleling the stream. Keeping a cautious lookout, we began to follow this road, slipping along through the timber at its side.

In about five minutes we came to a coal mine on the slope beside the highway. From the looks of its dump, it was being worked constantly—probably furnishing the fuel to keep fire under the *Nippon's* boilers.

Fifteen more minutes passed in laborious climbing over rocks and fallen timber, when all at once, after ascending a slight rise to another level of the valley's floor, we beheld the lights of a village a short distance beyond! At once Dr. Gresham changed our course to take us up the mountainside, whence we could look down upon the settlement.

To my amazement, we saw a neatly laid out town of more than a hundred houses, with electric-lighted streets. Although the houses seemed to be built entirely of corrugated sheet iron—probably because a more substantial type of construction would not have withstood the earthquakes—there was about the place an indefinable Chinese atmosphere.

My first shock of surprise at coming across this hidden city soon gave way to wonder that the outside world knew nothing of such a place —that it was not even indicated on the maps. But I recalled that on the land side it was unapproachable because of lofty mountains, beyond which lay an immense trackless wilderness; and on the water side it was a hundred miles off even the navigation lanes to Alaska.

Suddenly, as we stood there in the timber, a deep-toned bell began to toll on the summit of the low mountain above us.

"The Temple of the Moon God!" exclaimed Dr. Gresham.

With the sounding of the bell, the village awakened into life. From nearly every house came figures clad in flaming orange costumes, exactly like the ones Dr. Gresham and I wore beneath our outer suits. At the end of the town these figures mingled and turned into a roadway, and a few moments later we saw they were coming up the hill directly toward us!

Not knowing which way they would pass, we crouched in the dark and waited.

Still the weird, mellow tocsin sounded above us—slowly, mystically, flooding the valley with somber, thrilling sound.

All at once we heard the tramping of many feet, and then perceived with alarm that the roadway up the mountainside passed not more than twenty feet from where we lay! Along it the silent, strange procession was mounting the slope!

"The Seuen-H'sin," whispered my companion, "on their way to the hellish temple rites!"

Scarcely breathing, we pressed flat upon the ground, fearful each instant we might be discovered. For a period that seemed interminable the brilliantly clad figures continued to shuffle by—hundreds of them. But at last there was an end of the marchers.

Immediately Dr. Gresham rose and, motioning me to follow his example, quickly slipped off his blue outer costume and rolled it into a small bundle, which he tucked under his arm. I was ready an instant later.

Creeping out to the road, we peered about to make certain no stragglers were approaching; then we hurried after the ascending throng. It was only a few moments until we overtook the rear ranks, whereupon we adopted their gait and followed silently, apparently attracting no attention.

The mountain was not very high, and at last we came out upon a spacious level area at the top. It was moderately well illuminated by electric lamps, and at the eastern end, near the edge of the eminence, we beheld a stone temple into which the multitude was passing. Depositing our rolls of outer clothing in a spot where we could easily find them again, we moved forward.

As we crossed the walled mountaintop, or temple courtyard it might be called, I swiftly took in the strange surroundings. The temple was a thing to marvel at. It was all of stone, with high, fantastically carved walls and an imposing façade of rounded columns. On each side of the central structure were wings, or side halls, that ran off into the darkness; and in front of these were walled courtyards with arched gateways, roofed with golden-yellow tiles. The structure must have required engineering skill of the highest order for its building, yet it appeared old, incredibly old, as if the storms of centuries had beaten upon it.

Everywhere about the walls were cracks—doubtless the result of the earthquakes—so numerous and pronounced that one wondered how the building held together.

Presently, as we advanced, I noticed an overturned and broken statue of Buddha, the stone figure partly overgrown with moss and lichens. As I studied this I recalled the bit of history Dr. Gresham had related to me a couple of days before as we journeyed northward on the *Albatross*—of the Chinese navigators, directed by Huei-Sen, a Buddhist monk, who had come "somewhere to the north" in the year 499 A. D. And I wondered if this was, indeed, the "Country of the Great Han" that was discovered by these Orientals in the long ago—if this might be one of the temples which Huei-Sen and his followers had built in the days a thousand years before Columbus.

I whispered these questions to the doctor.

With an alarmed glance about us to make sure I had not been overheard, he answered very low:

"You have guessed it! But keep silent, as you value your life! Stay close to me and do whatever the others do!"

We were now at the entrance to the temple. Heavy yellow curtains covered the portal, and within a gong droned slowly.

Summoning courage, we pushed aside the draperies and entered.

The place was large and dimly lighted. Low red seats ran crosswise in long rows. At the far end, against the east wall, was the altar, before which were drawn deep yellow hangings. In front of these, under a hood of golden gauze, burned a solitary light. There was a terror in this mysterious dusk that gave me a strange thrill.

The audience was standing, silent, with bowed heads, by the rows of seats. Quaking inwardly, we took places in the last row, where the light was dimmest. So perfectly were our costumes and make-up a match for those around us that we attracted no attention.

All at once the tempo of the gong's droning changed, becoming slower and weirder, and other gongs joined in at intervals. The illumination, which appeared to come solely from the ceiling, brightened somewhat.

Then a door opened on the right, about midway of the building, and there appeared a being such as I had never beheld before. He was tall and lean and wore a robe of golden silk. Behind him came another—a priest in superb violet; and behind him a third in flaming orange. They wore high helmets with feathery plumes.

In the hands of each priest were peculiar instruments—or images, if so they might be called. Above a handle about two feet long, held vertically, was a thin rod curved upward in a semi-circle, at each end of which was a flat disk about a foot in diameter—one disk of silver, the other of gold. As I scrutinized these emblems I wondered if they were meant to symbolize the Seuen-H'sin's belief in two moons.

Slowly the priests advanced to a central aisle, then forward to an open space, or hall of prayer, before the altar.

Then a door opened on the left, opposite the first portal, and from it issued a fourth priest in robes of richest purple, followed by another in crimson, and still another in wondrous green. They, also, wore the high, feathery helmets and carried the instruments with gold and silver disks.

When the last three had joined the first trio, other portals opened along the sides of the temple, and half a dozen more priests entered and strode forward. The brilliant colors of their frocks seemed a part of the devilish gong-droning. In the dim vastness of the temple they moved on, silent as ghosts. There was something singularly depressing in the slow, noiseless steps. It was as if they were walking to their death.

Still the procession grew in numbers. Hitherto unnoticed portals gave entrance to more yellow, orange and violet-clad priests—demoniacal-looking beings, with lean, cruel, thoughtful faces and somber, dreaming eyes.

At last the procession ended. There was a pause, after which the audience standing among the rows of red seats burst into low murmurs of supplication. Sometimes the voices rose into a considerable humming sound; again they sank into a whisper. Suddenly the murmur of voices ceased and there was a blare of unseen trumpets—a crashing vastness of sound; harsh, unearthly, infernal, so that I shivered in horror. Nothing could be seen of the terrible orchestra; its notes seemed to come from a dark adjoining hall.

Again there was a pause—a thrilling period in which even the droning gongs were hushed; and then from an unseen portal came, slowly and alone, a figure that all the rest seemed to have been waiting for.

Leaning close to my ear, Dr. Gresham whispered:

"The high priest, Kwo-Sung-tao!"

With leaping interest, I turned to view the personage—and was held spellbound by the amazing personality of this man who proposed to make himself emperor of all the world.

He was old, *old;* small, shrunken; a very mummy of a man; bald, and with a long white mustache; enveloped in a shroud of cloth of gold, embroidered with crimson dragons and dual gold and silver moons. But never to my dying day can I forget that face, with its fearful eyes! All the wisdom and power and wickedness of the world were blended there.

Straight toward the altar the old man walked, looking neither to the right nor the left; and when he had mounted the steps he paused before the curtains and turned. As his blazing eyes swept the hall the entire multitude seemed to shrink and shrivel. An awful, sepulchral silence fell upon the crowd. The stillness hovered like a living thing. A thrill more intense than I had ever felt came over me; it swept me on cold waves into an ocean of strange, pulsing emotion.

Then, abruptly, a hundred cymbals clashed, subdued drums rolled forth, and the infernal trumpets that had heralded the entrance of the high priest crashed out a demoniacal peal—a veritable anthem of damnation that pierced me to the marrow.

The sound died out. The lights, too, began to sink. For a few moments not a word was spoken; there was the stillness of death, of the end of things. Presently all the illumination was gone save the solitary hooded light in front of the altar.

From his place at the head of the steps the high priest, Kwo-Sung-tao, made a gesture. Silently, and by unseen means, the deep yellow hangings rolled away.

There, to my amazement, the whole end of the temple was open, and we could look off from the mountaintop across innumerable valleys to the great range of peaks that walled the east. Out there the stars were shining, and near the horizon the blue-green heavens were tinged with a swimming silver mist.

The altar itself, if such it might be called, was a single block of undraped stone, about three feet high and four feet long, rising in the center of the platform.

Hardly had I taken in the scene before two of the priests hurried forward, dragging between them a nearly-naked and half-swooning Chinese girl. Carrying her up the steps, they flung her on her back upon the altar block and swiftly fastened her hands and feet to manacles on the sides of the stone, so that her naked breast was centered upon the pedestal. The priests then descended from the altar, leaving Kwo-Sung-tao alone beside the prisoner.

Still within the temple the profound silence reigned. There was not a whisper, not a rustle of the silken vestments.

But all at once we noticed that the eastern sky was growing brighter.

Then from before the altar a single somber bass rolled forth in a wailing prayer—a mystical, unearthly sound, coming in shattered sobs:

"Na-mo O-mi-t'o-fo! Na-mo O-mi-t'o-fo!"

Suddenly, from over the edge of the world, the moon began to rise!

This was the signal for another hellish blast from the trumpets, followed by the beginning of a steady humming of countless gongs. Other voices joined the quivering bass, together growing louder—seeming to complain and sob and wail like the voices of tortured demons in the abyss.

The rhythmic sounds swelled louder and louder, higher and higher, until the orb of night had climbed clear of the wall of mountains.

Directly against the silver disk I now saw silhouetted the stone altar holding its shrinking prisoner, with the high priest standing close beside her. The priest's right arm was upraised, and in his hand there gleamed a knife.

Still the music grew in volume—tremendous, stunning, a terrific battle of sound.

All at once the high priest's knife flashed downward—straight and deep into the breast of the quivering wretch upon the stone—and in a moment his other hand was raised in salutation to the moon, and in it was clutched the dripping heart of the human sacrifice!

At the sight my limbs grew shaky and my senses swam.

But at this instant, like a blow upon the head, came a lightning-crash of cymbals, a smiting of great gongs, and a climacteric roar from those agonizing trumpets of hell. Then even the single altar light went out, plunging the great hall into darkness.

Instantly I felt Dr. Gresham's hand upon my arm, and, dazed and helpless, I was dragged out of the temple.

Outside the air released me from my stupor, and I raced beside the scientist to the spot where we had left our outer garments. In the shadow of the wall we slipped these on, and then fled panic-stricken down the mountainside.

CHAPTER 8
THE JAWS OF DEATH

WE DID not pause in our flight from the temple until we reached the foot of the mountain; then, still shaken by the horror of the scene we had witnessed, we sat down to rest until the climbing moon should send its light into the depths of the gorge.

We could discern little of our surroundings, but close at hand we could hear the river rushing between its rocky walls.

Not a word was spoken until finally I inquired: "What next?"

In a low voice that indicated the need of caution even here, Dr. Gresham announced:

"The real work of the night still is before us. I would not have taken the risk of visiting the temple but for the hope that we would learn more of the Seuen-H'sin's layout than we did. Since nothing was gained there, we must reconnoiter the country."

"That sacrifice of human life," I asked— "what was its purpose?"

"To propitiate their god," the astronomer told me. "Every month, on the night of the full moon—in every Seuen-H'sin temple in the world—that hideous slaughter takes place. At certain times the ceremony is elaborated into a thing infinitely more horrible."

76

At this juncture the moon lifted itself clear of the valley's eastern rim, and the depression was bathed in silvery radiance. This was the signal for our start.

Heading toward the sound of the river, we soon came to the road that led to the *Nippon's* wharf. Beside this highway was an electric transmission line, running on up into the canyon. Turning away from the wharf and the village, we proceeded to follow this line toward its source.

Instead of traversing the road, however, we kept in the shadows of the timber at its side; and it was well that we did so, for we had not gone far before a group of Chinamen appeared around a bend in the highway, walking rapidly toward the town. They wore dark clothes of the same pattern as our own outer garments; and they passed without seeing us.

For fully two miles we followed the power line, until we began to pass numerous groups of Chinamen in close succession—like crowds of men getting off work.

To diminish the chance of our being discovered, Dr. Gresham and I turned up the mountainside. We climbed until we had reached a considerable height above the floor of the gorge, and then, keeping at this elevation, we again pursued the course of the electric line.

Another half-hour passed in this scramble along the steep slope, and my companion began to betray uneasiness lest the road and its paralleling copper wires, which we could not see from here, had ended or had turned off up some tributary ravine—when suddenly there came to our ears a faint roaring, as of a distant waterfall. At once Dr. Gresham was all alertness, and with quickened steps we pressed forward in the direction of the sound.

Five minutes later, as we rounded a shoulder of the mountain, we were stricken suddenly speechless by the sight, far below us, of a great, brilliantly lighted building.

For a few moments we could only stand and gaze at the thing; but presently, as the timber about us partly obstructed our view, we moved forward to a barren rocky promontory jutting out from the mountainside.

The moon now was well up in the heavens, and from the brow of this headland a vast expanse of country was visible, its every feature standing out almost as clearly as in the daylight. But, to take advantage of this view, we were obliged to expose ourselves to discovery by any spies the Seuen-H'sin might have posted in the region. The danger was considerable, but our curiosity regarding the lighted building was sufficient to outweigh our caution.

The structure was too far distant to reveal much to the naked eye, so we quickly brought our field glasses into use; then we saw that the building was directly upon the bank of the river, and that from its lower wall spouted a number of large, foaming streams of water, as if discharged under terrific pressure. From these torrents, presumably, came the sound of the waterfall. The angle at which we were looking down upon the place prevented our seeing inside the building except at one corner, where, through a window, we could catch a glimpse of machinery running.

But, little as we could see, it was enough to convince me that the place was a hydro-electric plant of enormous proportions, producing energy to the extent of probably hundreds of thousands of horsepower.

Even as I was reaching this conclusion, Dr. Gresham spoke:

"There," he said, "is the source of the Seuen-H'sin's power, which is causing all these upheavals throughout the world! That is where the yellow devils are at work upon their second moon!"

Just as he spoke another of the great ground shocks rocked the earth. Too much amazed for comment, I stood staring at the plant until my companion added:

"There is where those brilliant flashes in the heavens came from last night. They were due to some accident in the machinery, causing a short circuit. For two nights I had been circling over this entire range of mountains in the hydroplane, in search of the sorcerers' workshop. The flashes were a fortunate circumstance that led me to the place."

"At last I understand," I remarked presently, "why you were so deeply interested, back there in Washington, in the steamship *Nippon* and the electric plant she was transporting to Hongkong. I suppose that is where the sorcerers obtained all this machinery!"

"Precisely!" agreed the astronomer. "That morning in Washington, when I got you to look up the inventory of the *Nippon's* cargo,

I had this solution of the mystery in mind. I knew from my years in Wu-yang that electricity was the force the sorcerers would employ, and I was certain I had seen mention in the newspapers of some exceptionally large electrical equipment aboard the *Nippon*. Those supposed pirates of the Yellow Sea were in reality the murderous hordes of the Seuen-H'sin, who had come out to the coast after this outfit."

"But why," I asked, "should these Chinamen, whose development of science is so far in advance of our own, have to get machinery from an inferior people? I should think their own appliances would have made anything from the rest of the world seem antiquated."

"You forget what I told you that first night we spoke of the Seuen-H'sin. Their discoveries never were backed up by manufacturing; they possessed no raw materials or factories or industrial instincts. They did not need to make machinery themselves. In spite of their tremendous isolation, they were watching everything in the outside world. They knew they could get plenty of machinery ready-made, once they had perfected their method of operations."

I was still staring at the monster power plant below us when Dr. Gresham announced:

"I know now that my theory of the earthquakes' origin was correct, and if we get back to the *Albatross* the defeat of the sorcerers' plans is assured."

"Tell me one thing more," I put in. "Why

did the Chinamen come so far from their own country to establish their plant?"

"Because," the doctor replied, "this place was so well hidden—yet so easy to reach. And the farther they came from their own country to apply their electric impulses to the earth, the less danger their native land would run."

"Still, for my part, the main point of the whole problem remains unsolved," I asserted. "How do the sorcerers use this electricity to shake the world?"

"That," replied the scientist, "requires too long an explanation for the present moment. On the way back to the ship I will tell you the whole thing. But now I must get a closer view of Kwo-Sung-tao's strange workshop."

As Dr. Gresham was speaking, some unexplained feeling of uneasiness—perhaps some faint sound that had registered itself upon my subconscious thoughts without my ears being aware of it—led my gaze to wander over the mountainside in our vicinity. As my eyes rested for a moment upon some rocks about a hundred yards away, I fancied I saw something stir at the side of them.

At this moment Dr Gresham made a move to leave the promontory. Laying a detaining hand swiftly upon his arm, I whispered:

"Wait! Stand still!"

Unquestioningly the astronomer obeyed; and for a couple of minutes I watched the neighboring clump of rocks out of the corner of my eye. Presently I saw a darkly clad figure crawl out of the shadow of the pile, cross a patch of moonlight, and join two other figures at the edge of the timber. The trio stood looking in our direction a moment, while apparently holding a whispered conference. Then all three disappeared into the shadow of the woods.

Immediately I announced to my companion:

"We have been discovered! There are three Chinamen watching us from the timber, not a hundred yards away!"

The scientist was silent a moment. Then:

"Do they know you saw them?" he asked.

"I think not," I replied.

Still without looking around, he asked:

"Where are they—directly behind us?"

"No; well to the side—the side nearest the power plant."

"Good! Then we'll move back toward the timber at once—go leisurely, as if we suspected nothing. If we reach the cover of the woods all right, we'll make a dash for it. Head straight up for the top of the ridge—cross over and descend into the gulch on the other side—then detour back toward the *Albatross*. Stick to the shadows—travel as fast as we can—and try to throw off pursuit!"

Moving off as unconsciously as if we were totally unaware that we had been observed, we struck out for the timber—all the time keeping a sharp lookout, for we half expected the spies to head us off and attempt a surprise attack. But we reached the darkness of the woods without even a glimpse of the Celestials; and instantly we broke into a run.

The ascent was too steep to permit much speed; moreover, the roughness of the ground

and the fallen timber hampered us greatly—
yet we had the consolation of knowing that it
equally hampered our pursuers.

For nearly an hour we pressed on. The
mountaintop was crossed, and we descended
into a canyon on the other side. No sight or
sound of the Chinamen had greeted us. Could
they have surmised the course we would take,
and calmly let us proceed, while they returned
for reinforcements to head us off? Or were
they silently stalking us to find out who we
were and whence we came? We could not
tell. And there was the other chance, too,
that we had shaken off pursuit.

Gradually this latter possibility became a
definite hope, which grew as our overtaxed
strength began to fail. Nevertheless, we pushed
on until we were so spent and winded that we
could scarcely drag one foot after the other.

We had now reached a spot where the floor
of the canyon widened out into a tiny level
park. Here the timber was so dense that we
were swallowed up in almost complete darkness; and in this protecting mantle of shadow
we decided to stop for a brief rest. Stretching
out upon the ground, with our arms extended
at our sides, we lay silent, inhaling deep breaths
of the cool, refreshing mountain air.

We were now on the opposite side of a long
and high mountain ridge from the Chinese
village, and, as nearly as we could estimate,
not more than a mile or two from the *Albatross*.

Lying there on the ground, we could feel
the earthquakes with startling violence. We
noticed that they no longer occurred only at

intervals of eleven minutes and a fraction—although they were particularly severe at those periods—but that they kept up an almost continuous quivering, as if the globe's internal forces were bubbling restlessly.

Suddenly, in the wake of one of the heavier shocks of the eleven-minute period, the intense stillness was broken by a sharp report, followed by a ripping sound from the bowels of the earth, that seemed to start close at hand and rush off into the distance, quickly dying out. From the mountainside above us came the crash of a falling tree and the clatter of a few dislodged rocks bounding down the slope. The earth swayed as if a giant gash had opened and closed within a few rods of us.

The occurrence made Dr. Gresham and me sit up instantly. Nothing, however, was visible through the forest gloom of any changes in the landscape. Again silence settled about us.

Several minutes passed.

Then abruptly, from a short distance away, came the sound of something stirring. Sitting motionless, alert, we listened. Almost immediately we heard it again, and this time the sound did not die out. Something off there in the timber was moving stealthily toward us!

Dropping back at full length upon the ground, with only our heads raised, we kept a sharp watch.

Only a few more moments were we kept in suspense; then, across a slit of moonlight, we saw five Chinamen swiftly moving. They were slinking along almost noiselessly, as if following a scent—and, with a shock, we

realized that it was ourselves they were track-
ing! We had not shaken off our pursuers,
after all!

Even before we could decide, in a whispered
debate, what our next move should be, our
nerves again were whipped taut by other sounds
close at hand—but now on the opposite side of
the little valley from the first ones. This time
the sounds grew fainter—only to become louder
again almost immediately, as if the intruders
were searching back and forth across the flat.
In a short while it became plain that they were
drawing closer to us.

"What fools we were to stop to rest!" the
astronomer complained.

"I have a hunch we would have run into
some of those spies if we had kept on," I
rejoined. "They must have headed us off
and found that we didn't pass on down this
canyon, else they wouldn't be searching here
so thoroughly.

"Right!" my friend agreed. "And now
they've got us in a tight place!"

"Suppose," I suggested, "we slip across the
valley and climb part-way up that other mountainside—then try to work along through the
timber up there until we're near the ship."

"Good!" he assented. "Come on!"

Lying at full length upon the ground and
wriggling along like snakes, we headed between
two groups of the searchers. It was slow
work, but we did not dare even to rise to our
knees to crawl. Twice we dimly made out, not
fifty feet away, some of the Chinamen slinking
along, apparently hunting over every foot of

the region. We could not tell how many of them there were now.

After a time that seemed nearly endless we reached the edge of the flat. Here we rose to our feet to tackle the slope in front of us.

As we did so, two figures leaped out of the gloom close at hand and split the night with cries of *"Fan kuei! Fan kuei!"* ("Foreign devils!")

Then they sprang to seize us.

Further concealment being impossible, we darted back into the valley, no longer avoiding the patches of moonlight, but rather seeking them, so that we could see where we were going. We were heading for the fiord.

In a few seconds other cries arose on all sides of us. It seemed that we were surrounded and that the whole region swarmed with Chinamen. Dark forms began to plunge out of the woods ahead to intercept us; the leading ones were not sixty feet away.

"We'll have to fight for it!" called Dr. Gresham. And our hands flew to our revolvers.

But before we could draw the weapons a great ripping and crashing sound burst forth upon the mountainside above us—the terrifying noise of rocks splitting and grinding—an appalling turmoil! Terrified, pursued and pursuers alike paused to glance upward.

There, in the brilliant moonlight, we saw a monster avalanche sweeping downward, engulfing everything in its way!

Abandoning the astronomer and me, the Chinamen turned to flee farther from the path of the landslide, and we all began running together down the valley.

Only a few steps had we gone, however, when above the roaring of the avalanche a new sound rang out—short, sharp, booming, like the report of a giant gun.

As I glanced about through the blotches of moonlight and shadow, I saw several of the sorcerers just ahead suddenly halt, stagger and then drop from sight.

Dr. Gresham and I stopped instantly, but not before we beheld other Chinamen disappearing from view.

The earth had opened and they were falling in!

Even as we stood there, hesitating, the black maw yawned wider—to our very feet—and with cries of horror we tried to stagger back. But we were too late. The sides of the crack were crumbling in, and in another instant the widening gash overtook us.

As his eyes met mine, I saw the astronomer topple backward and disappear.

A second later the ground gave way beneath my own feet and I was plunged into the blackness of the pit.

CHAPTER 9
IN THE SORCERER'S POWER

WHAT happened immediately after that first drop into the abyss I do not know. My only recollection is of hurtling down a steep incline amid a smothering avalanche of dirt, of striking heavily upon a rocky ledge, and of bounding off again into the inky void as my senses left me.

The next thing I knew was the slow dawn of a sensation of cold; and then my eyes fluttered open and I beheld the moon shining upon me through a rent in the surrounding blackness. At first I was too much dazed to comprehend anything that had occurred, but soon, with considerable pain, I raised myself upon one elbow and looked about, whereupon understanding gradually returned.

The place where I lay was a mud-covered ledge upon one of the steep, sloping walls of a huge chasm that had opened in the earth. The gash was probably seventy-five feet across at this point, and above me the walls soared perhaps a hundred feet. Within arm's reach the shelf that supported me broke off in a precipice. I was half imbedded in soft mud, and was soaked to the skin and nearly frozen.

How long I had lain there I could not tell, but I judged it had not been more than two or three hours, for the moon still was high in the heavens.

All at once, as I gazed upon the weird scene, my heart leaped with anguish at remembrance of my vanished comrade, Dr. Ferdinand Gresham. He had dropped before me into the chasm, and therefore must have fallen clear of the ledge and plunged into the depths!

Thrusting myself to the edge of the precipice, I peered below. Nothing rewarded my gaze except horrifying silence and vapory gloom. The pain of the movement was so intense that I fell back almost in a swoon.

Before long, however, I saw that the moon was drawing near the rim of the gorge and that I should soon be engulfed in utter darkness, so I turned my eyes up the jagged wall in search of some means of escape. After considerable study, I thought I could discern a way to the summit.

But just then another surprise caught my gaze: the strip of sky above the chasm appeared narrower than when I had first turned my eyes upward. For a few moments I attributed this fact to an optical illusion produced by swiftly moving clouds overhead; but all at once the hideous truth burst upon me—*the crack in the earth was drawing shut!*

Heedless of the pain, I flung myself against the cliff—climbing in utter panic, for fear the chasm would close completely before I could get out.

The ascent was difficult and perilous in the extreme. Often rocks loosened beneath my fingers, starting miniature avalanches, and I flattened myself against the wall in a paroxysm of terror and clung there until the danger passed.

For a space that seemed hours long I continued to claw my way upward—with the prodigious trap closing steadily upon me. At times I found myself below unscalable surfaces, and was obliged to descend a bit and start over again in a new direction; and often it seemed as if the pain of my injuries would cause me to faint.

When I had come within thirty feet of the top, the climb developed into a veritable race with death, for the opposite wall was now almost upon me.

And then, suddenly, I found the way blocked by a sheer, unscalable wall, upon which only a fly could have found a foothold! Simultaneously I saw that the moon was right at the rim of the chasm, and that in a minute the light would vanish.

With the realization of my plight, panic seized me, and I beat my head against the wall and shrieked aloud.

And, though I could not guess it then, that very outcry of despair was to save my life.

Hardly had my first shriek gone forth before a head appeared directly above me, and a voice rang out:

"Here he is, fellows! Quick with that rope!"

With leaping heart, I recognized the voice as Dr. Gresham's!

An instant later a rope with a loop in the end of it dangled beside me, and a number of hands reached out to pull me to safety. An-

other moment, and I was drawn over the brink
—not one second too soon, for as I made the
last dozen feet the closing walls of the pit
brushed my body.

Exhausted and trembling, I sank upon the
ground, while a number of figures crowded
about me. These proved to be twenty-five
men from the *Albatross,* under command of
Ensign Wiles Hallock. They were all dressed
in the dark blue garments of the sorcerers.

How they came to be there was briefly related
by Dr. Gresham.

When the ground had opened beneath us
earlier in the evening, the astronomer had
clutched the roots of a tree, and within a few
seconds after I had dropped from sight he
was back on firm ground. The Chinamen who
had been pursuing us had either fallen into
the gash or had fled in terror.

Considerable vapor was rising from the pit,
but the scientist noticed that this was clearing
rapidly, so he decided to linger at the spot
awhile, with the forlorn hope that I might be
found. Soon the vapor vanished and, as the
moonlight was shining directly into the crack,
the doctor began a search.

After a time he discerned a figure lying upon
a ledge below. Close scrutiny revealed that
the dark costume characteristic of the Seuen-
H'sin was torn, displaying an orange garment
beneath.

Confident that none of the sorcerers would
be wearing two suits at once in this fashion,
the scientist concluded the figure was mine.
For a time he doubted whether I lived, but

eventually he thought he saw me stir feebly, whereupon he began frantic efforts to reach me.

Repeated attempts to descend the precipice failed. Then he tried dropping pebbles to arouse me. Again unsuccessful, he risked attracting the sorcerers back to the spot by shouting into the chasm.

All his efforts proved futile, so he finally returned to the destroyer and obtained this rescue party.

In grateful silence I gripped his hand.

"Now," the astronomer concluded, "if you are able to walk, we will get back to the ship. It is only 1 o'clock, and if we hurry there still is time to attack the Seuen-H'sin before daylight. Conditions throughout the world are so alarming that we must put this power plant out of business without delay!"

"Go ahead!" I assented. "I'm able to hobble along!"

It was less than two miles to the destroyer's anchorage, they said. During the march none of the sorcerers was sighted, with which we began to conclude that the cracking of the earth had affected the village on the other side of the mountain so that all their lookouts had been called in.

But suddenly, when we were less than half a mile from the vessel, the stillness of the night was shattered by the shrill blast of a whistle. A series of other wild shrieks from the steam chant came in quick succession.

"The *Albatross!*" exclaimed Ensign Hallock. "Something's happening!"

We burst into a run—the whistle still screaming through the night.

All at once the sound ceased, and as the echoes died out among the hills we heard the rattle of firearms.

"An attack!" cried Hallock. "The sorcerers have attacked the ship!"

Then, abruptly, the firing, too, died out.

A few moments later we emerged from the ravine onto the bank of the fiord and into full view of the destroyer. The passing of the moon into the west had brought the vessel within its rays—and the sight that greeted us almost froze our blood!

Swarming about the deck were dozens of Chinamen—some with rifles, some with knives. They appeared to be completely in control of the ship. Numerous pairs of them were coming up from below decks, carrying the bodies of the vessel's crew, which they carelessly tossed overboard. Evidently they had taken our companions by surprise and wiped them out!

At this sight Ensign Hallock and his men became frenzied with rage.

"Ready, men!" the officer announced to his followers. "We're going down there and give those murderers something to remember!"

Eagerly the seamen prepared to charge the ship. But Dr. Gresham stopped them.

"It's no use," he said. "There are hundreds of the sorcerers down there—and only a handful of us. You would only be throwing away your lives and defeating the whole purpose of this expedition. We must find a better way."

The astronomer's counsel prevailed, where-upon we debated what should be done. The situation was desperate. Here we were, completely isolated in a grim wilderness, hundreds of miles from help, and surrounded by hordes of savage fanatics. Soon, no doubt, the sorcerers' spies would find us. And meanwhile we were helpless to put an end to the terrors that were engulfing the planet and its inhabitants.

So despair gradually took possession of us. Not even the customary resourcefulness of Dr. Gresham rose to the emergency.

Suddenly Ensign Hallock gave an exclamation of excitement.

"The *Nippon!*" he burst out. "Let's turn the tables on the Chinese, and seize the *Nippon!* She probably has a guard on board, but maybe we can take it by surprise!"

"What could we do with her?" I objected. "She needs a large crew—and there are only twenty-seven of us!"

"We'll sail her away, of course!" replied the young naval officer with enthusiasm. "There must be fuel on board, for her fires are going. Three of the boys here are apprentice engineers. I can do the navigating. And the rest of you can take turns stoking the boilers!"

"But how could we slip past the *Albatross?*" asked Dr. Gresham.

Ensign Hallock seemed to have thought of that, too, for he promptly answered:

"The *Albatross* is an oil-burning craft, with the new type of burners that came into use since these Chinks have been stowed away here in the wilderness. The mechanism for using the oil is quite complicated, and the sorcerers are likely to have trouble operating her until they figure out the system. If we reach them before they have time to master the thing, they will be helpless to stop us!"

The young man's enthusiasm was contagious. Dr. Gresham began to give heed.

"Even if we fail to get away in the *Nippon,*" the scientist admitted, "she has a powerful wireless outfit: Kwo-Sung-tao has been using it to communicate with Washington. With that radio in our hands for ten minutes, we can summon help sufficient to annihilate these yellow devils!"

The plan was adopted without further question. And, believing that the sorcerer's easy victory over the *Albatross* had made them careless, perhaps, we struck out in as direct a course as possible for the spot at which the *Nippon* was docked.

In twenty minutes, without sighting any of the enemy, we arrived at the edge of the timber behind the wharf.

CHAPTER 10
WE TAKE DESPERATE CHANCES

THE great liner lay silent in the moonlight, with no lights visible about her, but thin columns of smoke rose lazily from her funnels. A gangplank was down.

It was decided that our number should divide into three equal parts. One was to go to the bow and board the craft there by climbing up the line fastening the ship to the pier; this line was in the shadow except at its far end, where the men would emerge upon the deck. The second group was to get aboard at the stern by the same means. And the third detachment was to advance by the gangplank.

The plan worked without a hitch, and soon we were assembled upon the vessel's main deck. No guard was in sight. Hurriedly we explored the upper decks and all the chambers off them. They were empty.

Then, descending simultaneously by companionways forward, aft, and amidship, we began to search the body of the vessel. Still no one could be found.

And this deserted condition of the ship continued until only the stokehold remained to be entered. Here, however, we were certain of finding people.

Leaving three men on deck to guard against surprise, the rest of us crept into the boiler room.

Only two Chinamen were in the place, leisurely engaged in stoking the furnaces. We had them covered with our revolvers before they had any warning of our approach.

In spite of the odds against them, one of the Mongolians leaped forward and had almost struck one of our men with his shovel before a shot killed him in his tracks. The other Chinaman submitted, and he at once was securely bound and dumped into a corner.

Dr. Gresham tried to question the prisoner in Chinese, but all the information he could get regarding the keeping up of steam on the *Nippon* was: "Maybe leave here soon!"

While the astronomer had been thus engaged, Ensign Hallock and some of his men were examining the coal bunkers, and they now reported that the vessel was stocked with fuel for a long voyage.

At this juncture, one of the deck watch came to announce that the moon was sinking near the mountaintops, and that if we hoped to get far down the channel before the light failed we would have to start promptly.

Detailing eighteen men to the firing—with orders to get more steam as rapidly as possible —Ensign Hallock and the rest of us rushed to the engine room, where the three apprentice engineers already were at work. Finding everything all right there, the officer proceeded to the steering-room, while some of us pulled in the gangplank.

The astronomer and I next started to find
the radio plant, to get into communication with
the Mare Island navy yard. But here we
encountered a setback: the wireless plant had
been removed! Kwo-Sung-tao, we could only
surmise, had moved the set to a spot more
convenient to the village. So, for the present,
communication with the outside world was
impossible.

During this brief period of putting the ship
in sailing order, none of the sorcerers made an
appearance; probably all the men they could
spare were exploring the captured destroyer.

Soon steam was up; whereupon Ensign
Hallock sent Dr. Gresham to the bow and
me to the stern to keep a close lookout, and
himself ascended to the bridge and gave the
order to start the engines and cast off. Before
many moments the leviathan was moving away
from the wharf.

The officer had found from the charts that
there was a place only half a mile or so up-
stream where the fiord opened into a bay. There,
from all indications, room might be had to
turn the ship around and head her down the
channel. For this opening he now set his course.

Although we maintained a very slow speed,
it was not long before we nosed our way into
the bay. Here the walls of the fiord retreated
far enough to form a considerable body of
water; nevertheless, it was plain we would
have close work turning the *Nippon* in such
a space. It would be necessary to steam well
over against the north bank, where there no

longer was any moonlight and the shore line was swallowed up in inky blackness.

Redoubling the vigilance of our lookout, we began the maneuver. Slowly Ensign Hallock swung the huge ship around. Twice it was necessary to stop and reverse the engines, accomplishing part of the turn by backing. In doing so, we had a narrow escape from running into a rocky promontory in the dark.

But at last the liner's head was fairly about and the way seemed clear for our dash down the channel past the *Albatross*. As the officer signaled for more speed, all of us unconsciously steeled ourselves for the climax of our adventure.

But at that instant a deep-toned bell, sounding like the tocsin upon the Temple of the Moon God, began tolling in the distance. This was followed almost immediately by a series of sharp blasts from the whistle of the destroyer.

Now that we had completed the dangerous turn, my duties in the stern were finished, so I ran forward, joining Dr. Gresham, and together we climbed to the bridge.

"The Chinks must have discovered that their ship is gone!" was the greeting the young officer gave us.

He was hardly able to restrain his excitement; the prospect of a brush with the sorcerers seemed to give him great joy.

The steam chant and the tolling of the bell continued, as if intended for a general alarm.

"Must be getting their gang together!" the ensign remarked. "They'll be laying for us

now, but we'll give them a run for their
money!"

The liner now was beginning to get under
considerable headway.

"We're in dangerous quarters until we get
out of this stretch of darkness!" the officer
announced. "Here—you fellows each take a
pair of glasses! You, doctor, keep watch from
the starboard end of the bridge! You"—
indicating me—"go to the port side! Watch
like hawks!"

We started, but—the command had come
too late!

With a dull, long-drawn ripping sound from
her interior, the great liner suddenly staggered
and listed heavily to port! We were thrown
off our feet.

"Struck a rock!" Ensign Hallock shouted,
as he leaped up. And instantly be began
signaling frantically to stop the engines. Almost in the same breath he yelled: "Go below
—both of you—quick! See what damage has
been done!"

As we rushed down from the bridge we could
tell from the *feel* of things that the vessel's
progress had come to a stop: the *Nippon* was
stuck fast!

At the head of the stairs leading to the boiler
room we met the seamen, who had been doing
stoker duty, rushing up.

"You can't go down there!" they shouted.
"The whole bottom's torn out!"

Nevertheless, we leaped past them and continued below. But near the bottom of the
stairs we were brought up short. A few lights

still were burning, and in their feeble rays we could see huge foaming torrents pouring into the place. Already the floor was awash to a depth of two or three feet, and before we could take our eyes from the sight the flood seemed to rise several inches! At any moment the boilers might explode!

Up the steps we dashed madly.

As we reached the deck every one was hurrying aft. We joined in the rush.

The tolling of the temple bell and the shrieking of the destroyer's whistle continued in the distance: the Seuen-H'sin was preparing to take up our pursuit!

Then, before we could make another move, the vessel suddenly lurched backward and listed heavily to starboard, with her stern rising high out of the water. Then she began to nose forward under the waves.

The Nippon was sinking!

CHAPTER 11
A WILD NIGHT'S WORK

"Lower the boats!" yelled Ensign Hallock.

The coolness, readiness and energy of this young man in any emergency were an inspiration.

All of us flew to obey the command, our number dividing between the two boats nearest the stern. The liner was sinking so fast that in a few moments the boats would be afloat, anyway; nevertheless, we soon had our craft in the water.

"Take that canvas covering!" bawled the ensign. "We may need it for a sail!"

A sailor dragged the canvas into the boat, and we pushed off from the vessel.

The other party had encountered trouble with the davit-blocks, which occasioned a slight delay, and Hallock was just getting his boat into the water when——

With a terrific crash, the *Nippon's* boilers burst!

The huge craft broke in two amidship, the central portion of her decks leaping out of the water. The force of the explosion hurled Ensign Hallock and his men—life-boat and all —over the stern amid a hurricane of debris, while our own craft was flung bottom-up with great violence, scattering us all about in the water.

In an incredibly brief time the *Nippon* slipped from view under the waves, the swiftness of her sinking causing a violent suction that swept us into a whirlpool filled with timbers, broken boats and wreckage of all sorts.

Something heavy struck me on the head and knocked me almost senseless, but I clutched a floating object and hung on in a daze. Presently I heard voices calling not far away and, swimming toward them, I found a couple of men clinging to the life-boat. Others quickly began to join us—among them Dr. Gresham. Soon we had the boat righted and found it undamaged. Someone picked up some oars.

Then we began rowing about the scene of the wreck, shouting and keeping a lookout for other survivors. In this way we rescued seven more men—one of the last being Ensign Hallock, who was dazed from a bad cut on the head.

After a time, believing further search to be futile, we made our way to the north bank of the fiord.

There now were only fifteen of us left—twelve men having perished in the explosion. While we were roughly dressing the wounds of the injured, we began to hear shouts in Chinese from the other side of the water, but the width of the fiord here was such as to make the cries indistinct. As the voices did not draw nearer, we began to believe that the sorcerers possessed no small boats in which to cross to the scene of the wreck. This gave us a greater feeling of safety, since the only way the sorcerers could get at us for the present was by swimming; and not enough of them were likely to try to constitute a serious menace.

In the distance the whistling and bell-ringing had now died out.

Hastily conferring upon what should be done, we decided to stick to the life-boat and drop down the channel, hoping to get out of the country of the Seuen-H'sin before daylight. This course seemed feasible, since the whole north bank of the fiord—the side opposite the village—was now in shadow.

We started at once, rowing along silently, close to the shore. Occasionally we heard voices on the south bank, but we made no closer acquaintance with the Chinese.

As we drew near the *Albatross,* we muffled our oarlocks with bits of cloth torn from our clothing, and took every precaution against making a sound.

A few lights were burning upon the destroyer's deck, but otherwise she seemed deserted; possibly the Seuen-H'sin believed we had perished in the blowing up of the *Nippon,* and that they had nothing more to fear from intruders.

All at once, as we began to drop below the vessel, Ensign Hallock gave an order to cease rowing. Drawing us close together so we could hear his whispered words, he announced:

"Boys, let's try to recapture the *Albatross!*"

Then, with repressed excitement, he unfolded a plan.

To our ears the ensign's words sounded like a proposal of suicide; but the situation was appallingly desperate, and the upshot of the matter was that we decided to make the attempt.

"Who is to go with you?" I asked Hallock.

Several of the men promptly volunteered, and the ensign selected a muscular seaman named Jim Burns.

Agreeing upon a signal that should inform us when to follow them, the officer and his partner slipped off most of their clothing and, arming themselves only with knives, swam away. In a few seconds they were lost from sight.

From Hallock himself, afterward, I learned the story of their daring undertaking—although I am certain he greatly minimized the dangers they ran.

Reaching the deep shadows beside the destroyer, Hallock and Burns swam forward to the anchor chain hanging from the bow. There they waited a time, but, hearing not a sound from above, the officer climbed up the chain and looked over the edge of the deck. No one was in sight.

He signaled Burns to come after him. Then, clinging to the edge of the deck, with their bodies dangling down the side of the hull, out of sight of any one above, they worked their way, hand over hand, back to a point opposite the after companionway. Still none of the Chinamen was in evidence.

The deck was lighted at this point and the rays of other electric lamps poured out of the open companionway; nevertheless, the men swung themselves up, climbed the rail, and darted to the side of the deck house. Leaving

Burns here, Hallock crept alone around the corner to the companionway.

Just as he reached the open door he almost collided with a Chinaman coming up the stairs!

Both were taken completely by surprise, but the ensign recovered quickest, and before there was time for an outcry he had the Mongolian by the throat and was choking the life out of him.

Soon the fellow crumpled limply upon the deck. Hallock drew his knife to finish the business—but at that instant there came the sound of voices approaching along the deck.

Seizing the unconscious Chinaman by the arms, Hallock dragged him swiftly around the corner of the deck house to where Burns was waiting.

Would the approaching men enter the companionway and go below, or come on back to the stern? In the latter case they were bound to discover the intruders.

With drawn knives, the two Americans stood ready; the success or failure of their whole enterprise depended upon the next few seconds.

But the Chinamen turned down the steps, and their voices soon died out in the interior of the vessel.

Thus assured of safety again for the moment, Ensign Hallock ended the career of the Mongolian and dragged the body into the deeper shadows in the stern. Then the two men advanced together to the companionway. Everything appeared quiet below.

Down the stairs they noiselessly crept. At the bottom they could faintly hear voices—

seemingly many of them—somewhere forward, or else on the next lower level. But they did not hesitate. The officer indicated the door of a compartment only a dozen feet away. They reached it and got inside.

The room had been converted, during this voyage, into a storeroom. Among its miscellaneous contents was a quantity of tear bombs —grenades that discharge a gas which makes the victim's eyes water until he is temporarily blinded and helpless. To obtain all these missiles they could carry was the work of but a few seconds, after which the Americans dashed for the steps and started to the deck.

Just as they got half-way up, a couple of Chinamen appeared suddenly in the passage below and caught sight of them. The Celestials uttered loud warning cries and darted after the visitors.

Instantly Seaman Burns, who was behind, hurled one of the bombs to the floor at the foot of the ladder—and then another, and another.

The sorcerers halted a moment, surprised by the missiles—and before they could resume their rush they were blinded by tears. Screaming in rage and dismay, they retreated down the passage toward the other voices that were beginning to respond to their cries.

With this, Burns ran on up to the deck.

"Stay here and hold this stairway!" ordered Hallock. "I'll go forward to the other ladder! Don't let any of them reach the deck!"

And the officer ran off.

He reached the forward companionway just as half a dozen of the Chinamen were crowding toward the foot of the stairs. A couple of the bombs hurled among them drove them back. Two more missiles followed; then Hallock slammed the door shut and fastened it.

Running to the rail, he signaled us to advance. In two or three minutes our rowboat was alongside and we were scrambling up the anchor chain.

On the main deck, under the bridge, formerly had been stored a number of rifles, and Hallock now ran to see if these were still there. Luckily the Chinamen had not disturbed them, and the officer soon was back with a loaded weapon for each man.

"The effect of the tear gas must be wearing off below," he announced, "so we can go down now and clean up those devils! But confine all your shooting under decks, where it's not so likely to be heard on shore!"

"And," interposed Dr. Gresham, "don't show a spark of mercy, or we will be certain to pay dearly for it later!"

Leaving six men on deck to keep watch, the rest of us divided and went down fore and aft. The gas still was strong, but no longer overpowering. The Chinese, we found, had groped their way into the engine room. Here we came upon them—forty-eight in all.

Upon the scene of slaughter that followed I will draw the veil. Thus the Seuen-H'sin had slain our comrades—and we knew that, were our positions now reversed, we should meet the same bloody end. Suffice it to say that within fifteen minutes the last of the sorcerers' bodies had been disposed of overboard.

Once more we were masters of the *Albatross!*

Our first move, we decided, would be to steam down the channel a few miles—where the Mongolians could not immediately get at us. Fortunately, two of the apprentice engineers were among the survivors, and they undertook to handle the machinery.

At the same time, Hallock and most of the crew went to work setting up rapid-fire guns in convenient places to repel invasion, and storing ammunition and hand grenades on deck. A couple of the larger guns likewise were unlimbered, ready for action.

By the time these tasks were completed, steam had been gotten up, and the vessel began its retreat down the channel.

Meanwhile, Dr. Gresham and I hastened to the radio room to summon aid from the Mare Island navy yard near San Francisco.

But barely had the astronomer placed the receivers to his ears and reached forward to adjust the apparatus, than a startling event forestalled his call.

CHAPTER 12
THE VOICE OF SCIENCE

AT THE precise instant when Dr. Gresham seated himself at the radio of the *Albatross,* the great Consolidated News Syndicate, which dealt with newspapers all over the world, was broadcasting a "flash" of terrible import:

An hour ago New York had been wiped out by a stupendous tidal wave!

Details of the disaster still were lacking.

And then, before the astronomer could lift a hand to send his call, some instantaneous and terrific disturbance of the atmosphere blotted out all wireless communication!

What this disturbance might be, or what it might portend, seemed to arouse in my companion the gravest alarm. His face looked ashen as he sat there at the key. Over and over he sought to get Mare Island, but without success: the ether was as unresponsive as if his instruments were dead.

Presently he rose without a word and, motioning me to follow, sought Ensign Hallock on the bridge. Briefly he told the young officer about the destruction of Manhattan, adding:

"Something serious has happened somewhere in the world, since then, completely to disorder the atmosphere. It may be the earth's final

110

struggle for existence. Unless the Seuen-H'sin's power is broken *at once,* the end is near! It is too late to wait for reinforcements. We must tackle the job ourselves—at any cost! The question is: how are we going to do it?

Hallock thought a few moments, and then replied:

"We can't bomb the place from an airplane, because we brought no airplane bombs. And we can't shell it with the ship's guns without knowing its exact location. Our planes aren't equipped with range finders, either—so it would do no good to try to locate it from the air.

"That," he added with decision, "leaves us no choice but a direct attack!"

"Well," responded Dr. Gresham, "at any cost, we've got to try!"

At once we consulted the ship's charts—and made a discovery.

Not far below our present location, a tributary fiord entered Dean Channel from the left, and with sudden hope we saw that this waterway twisted among the mountains for several miles—reaching a point in one of its windings where it was not more than six or seven miles directly south of the region in which the power plant was hidden.

"There's our chance!" Hallock announced. "If the sorcerers have missed the *Albatross,* they'll think we are on our way out of the country as fast as we can travel. They won't be expecting us to come back so soon—in broad daylight. We can steam up this side channel to the proper spot and then march across the mountains until we find the plant."

"Good!" assented the scientist. "They are less likely to be on guard against an attack from that side, anyway!"

Day was now beginning to break, which made further navigation easy. In a few minutes we came to the tributary inlet and swung the vessel in between its high, constricted walls.

The ensign was now imbued with marvelous activity. Orders flew thick and fast. A couple of the machine guns were made ready for land transport. Two light mountain mortars and a quantity of ammunition were brought up on deck. A supply of shrapnel hand grenades was distributed among the men.

Our progress through this tortuous waterway necessarily was slow; nevertheless, at the end of an hour, and a half, the destroyer was stopped and we made ready for the final adventure.

It was decided that all fifteen of us should go, because less than that number could not carry our equipment up and down the steep mountainsides, and three or four men left to guard the ship would be utterly useless in the event of an attack.

So with every nerve alert, we struck out through the trackless wilderness.

Three hours later we came upon six large steel conduits which we knew must convey the water power to the plant, and in a few minutes we had followed these to our goal.

Here we found ourselves upon the brow of

a promontory directly behind and fully 300 feet above the Seuen-H'sin's workshop. The promontory ended in a sheer precipice, from the outermost curve of which the conduits dropped straight down into the power house. This tremendous fall of the six streams of water supplied the enormous energy to the turbines. The summit of this projecting ridge was fairly level, and for a distance of perhaps seventy-five yards at the end the timber had been entirely cleared away.

Extending out from the brow of the precipice, and resting upon the tops of the conduits where they plunged downward, was a narrow bridge of iron lattice-work which connected all six of the pipes and gave access to the bolts which tightened the steel elbows. Through holes in this grating, iron ladders fastened between the pipes and the granite cliff back of them descended clear to the bottom of the precipice.

A slight rail only three feet high protected the outer edge of this grid—a little hand-hold for the workmen in case of a misstep. From this dizzy balcony it would be possible to drop a stone almost upon the roof of the power house.

After a quick look around, Ensign Hallock chose a spot a little back from the cliff to set up the mortars that were to throw explosives upon the building. He also prepared to place mines under the conduits. But first the machine guns were planted to command the surrounding timber, in case of an attack.

There still was no indication that the sorcerers suspected our presence in their vicinity; so, inasmuch as Hallock said his preparations would take some little time, Dr. Gresham determined to emply the interval in getting a closer look at the power plant.

One of the ladders down the precipice, he had noticed, was in such a position behind its water main that it could not be seen from the building, and he decided to attempt the approach by this means. To my delight, he made no objection to my accompanying him.

As we slipped through an opening in the iron bridge and started our dizzy descent of the ladder—which seemed to sway beneath our weight—I felt a thrill of exultation, in spite of our peril, at the thought that at last we were to solve the mystery of the Seuen-H'sin's terrible power over our planet!

The trip was slow and risky, but finally we came abreast of a window in the rear wall of the building, and by stretching around the side of the thick water main we could see into the place.

The workshop of the sorcerers was a long, low, narrow structure directly beside the river. Like the houses back in the Chinese village, it was a mere shell of corrugated iron, its steel framework so bolted together that it could sway with the earth tremors.

In a row down the center of the structure were six huge turbines, operating electric generators.

Along one side of the room was the largest switchboard I had ever seen, while the whole of the other lengthwise wall was flanked with

a series of massive induction coils, elaborately
insulated from each other and from the ground.
Although I knew little about electricity, I was
certain that if the combined electrical output
of those dynamos were directed through that
maze of coils, the resulting voltage could only
be measured in the millions—perhaps hundreds
of millions!

From one large, enclosed object, supported
on steel uprights over the row of induction
coils, two electric cables, more than two inches
in diameter, ran off through the north end of
the building. One of these ended in a tiny
structure about eighty yards from the power
house. The other ran on up the valley.

But, most curious of all, in the center of the
switchboards was an apparatus surmounted by
a large clock, before which a Chinese attend-
ant sat constantly. Precisely every eleven
minutes and six seconds a bell on this clock
clanged sharply, and there was a bright flash
in a long glass tube, followed by an earth
shock.

For some time we clung there in the shadows,
while Dr. Gresham studied every detail of the
amazing workshop. Then, calling my attention to the fact that the place outside the
power house, where one of the cables ended,
was hidden from view of the attendants inside
by a thick clump of trees, the astronomer said
he wanted a closer look at this place.

Creeping through the timber, we reached the
tiny structure over the cable's end. Not the
slightest watch seemed to be kept anywhere
about the plant. The door to the house was

not fastened, so we entered and looked hurriedly about.

The room was absolutely empty, except for the heavy cable, which came to the center of the floor and there connected with a copper post about four inches in diameter that ran straight down into the ground.

Without lingering further, we crawled back to the ladder and commenced our long climb up the cliff.

Upon reaching the top again, we found the ensign and his men still busy with their preparations for the bombardment. Withdrawing far enough to be out of their hearing, the astronomer turned to me and remarked:

"Well, what do you think of the scientific achievements of the sorcerers now?"

"I don't know what to think!" I replied. "It's utterly beyond my comprehension!"

The doctor chuckled at my dismay.

"Forgive me," he said, "for having kept you so long in the dark. Until today I could never prove my theories—certain as I was of their correctness—and I did not wish to attempt any explanations until I was sure of my ground. But now you have seen enough to understand the solution of the puzzle."

To my delight, the scientist was dropping into one of his most communicative moods. After a moment he went on:

"To comprehend, even in a general way, what the Seuen-H'sin has done, you must understand the principle of resonance.

"Let us start with the swinging pendulum of a clock. What keeps it in motion? Nothing but a slight push, delivered at exactly the right time. Any swinging object can be kept swinging, even though it weigh many tons, if it is given a touch by the finger of a baby at *just the right moment*. By the same principle, the amount of swing can be increased enormously if the successive pushes are correctly timed.

"But we need not limit our illustration to swinging objects. Everything in the world has a natural period of vibration, whether it be a violin string, or a battleship, or a forty-story skyscraper.

"Fifty men can capsize a twenty-thousand-ton battleship merely by running back and forth from one side of the deck to the other and carefully timing their trips to the vessel's rolling. A child with a tack-hammer can shake down a forty-story skyscraper if he can discover the natural period of the building's vibration and then tap persistently upon the steel framework at the correct intervals.

"Even the earth itself has its natural period of vibration.

"If you exploded a ton of dynamite on top of the ground it would blow quite a hole and jar the earth for several miles around it; and that would be all. But if you set off another ton of dynamite, and then another and another, and kept it up continuously—always timing the explosions to the period of the earth's vibration—eventually the jar would be felt clear through the globe. And if you still persisted, in time you would wreck the world.

"Such is the cumulative power of many little blows correctly timed. The principle of timing small impulses to produce large effects is the principle of resonance.

"But there are other forces in nature which can produce vibration—electricity, for instance. Nikola Tesla demonstrated a number of years ago that the globe is resonant to electric waves.

"Now, suppose some person constructed an apparatus that could suddenly turn a tremendous flood of electric waves into the earth. That energy would go clear through the globe, imparting a tiny impulse to every atom of matter of which the sphere is composed—like a push upon the pendulum of a clock.

"And suppose that person knew the exact period of the earth's vibration, and sent another bolt, and another and another, into the globe—all exactly timed to impart a fresh impulse at the correct moment—to give the pendulum another push, so to speak. Then let him pile electric impulse upon electric impulse, each at just the right second, until the accumulation of them all represented millions of horsepower in electric oscillations. In time, *the world would be shaken to pieces!*

"And—impossible as it sounds—that is the very principle the Seuen-H'sin is using there beneath your eyes! The dynamos furnish the power, and that great battery of induction coils magnifies it to an almost inconceivable voltage. By those cables attached to copper plugs, the impulses are conveyed to the earth.

"Every blow of that tremendous electric hammer is heavier than the preceding one because it has the accumulated power of all the others behind it. With every blow the earth grows weaker—less able to stand the shock. Continued, the planet's doom would be inevitable—if it is not already so!"

I had been listening to this recital with amazement too profound to admit of interruption. When Dr. Gresham finished I sat silent, turning it all over in my mind, and reflecting how simple the explanation seemed. Finally—

"Was it those electric waves being discharged into the ground," I asked, "that Professor Howard Whiteman in Washington mistook for wireless signals from Mars?"

"Precisely!" was the answer.

"And how," I inquired, "was it possible for the sorcerers to discover the exact period of the earth's vibration? That seems little short of superhuman."

"Doubtless you remember the newspaper accounts published that night when we returned from Labrador," replied the doctor. "They told how the electric whispers, when first noticed, occurred exactly two minutes apart; then the interval increased one minute each night until the signals were separated by more than thirty minutes; afterward the lulls altered erratically for some time, until they became fixed at eleven minutes and six seconds."

"Yes," I assented.

"Well," continued the scientist, "those variations simply denoted the experiment of the Seuen-H'sin to ascertain the period of the globe's vibration. If, after continuing their discharges all one night, their seismographs showed no response from the earth, they knew their bolts were wrongly timed, and they experimented with another period.

"Eventually they found that their impulses penetrated the earth with a speed of approximately 709 miles a minute—in other words, in precisely eleven minutes and six seconds the waves passed clear through the planet. This, then, was demonstrated to be the length of time that must elapse before the pendulum—figuratively speaking—could be given another electrical push. You saw just now, on the switchboard down there, the clockwork apparatus which times those bolts."

After a moment's consideration I remarked:

"Your own electrical equipment on board the *Albatross*—those big induction coils and the rest of it—what did you plan to do with that?"

"I had meant to fight the Seuen-H'sin with its own methods," the doctor replied. "I was going to throw a high-power electric current into the earth at intervals between those of the sorcerers'—say five minutes apart. That would have interfered with the acceleration of the vibrations—like setting a second group of men to run across the ship's deck between the trips of the first group. One set of vibrations would have neutralized the other.

"But," Dr. Gresham added, "the time for such methods is past. We must end the whole thing immediately—at one stroke!"

Receiving a signal from Ensign Hallock that he was ready, we started to rejoin the ship's party. But before we had gone a dozen steps we were rooted to the spot by a new terror!

Off in the east, where the snow-covered peaks lifted into the sky, suddenly burst forth an awful crashing sound, as of a colossal cannonade—a ponderous and unbroken thunderroll, terrible as the enormous tumult of the day of doom. As our gaze followed the nightmare sounds to the edge of the world we beheld the lofty mountains oscillate, crack, disjoint, and crumble into seething ruin.

The noise that accompanied this destruction came roaring and booming across the intervening miles—a stupendous and unearthly commotion, shattering the very atmosphere to fragments.

For a minute Dr. Gresham stood petrified. But as the enormity of the cataclysm became evident, an unconscious cry, almost a groan, escaped him:

"Too late! Too late! The beginning of the end!"

Suddenly he wheeled—almost livid with excitement—to the naval officer and screamed at the top of his voice:

"*Fire!* For God's sake destroy that power plant! *Fire! FIRE!*"

CHAPTER 13
PLAYING OUR FINAL CARD

IN THEIR astonishment at the terrible upheaval, Ensign Hallock and his men had left their posts and crowded toward the end of the promontory, a few feet away from the mortars. At Dr. Gresham's command to fire, most of them leaped to obey the order.

Instantly the woods behind us sprang into life as a horde of Chinamen dashed from cover, charging straight at us!

From the size of the attacking force, it was evident our presence had been known for some time and our capture delayed until a sufficient number of the sorcerers could be assembled to insure our defeat: there seemed to be scores of the blue-clad figures. Most of them were armed with rifles, although some had only knives and a few iron bars which they wielded as clubs.

The distance across the clearing was not much more than 200 feet, and the Chinamen advanced at a run—without any outcry.

But before they had traversed a quarter of the space Ensign Hallock recovered from his surprise and, with a few terse commands, led his crew into action. Dashing to the machine guns, the seamen threw themselves flat on the ground; and while some manned these weapons, the rest resorted to their revolvers. In two or three seconds the booming of the distant cataclysm was augmented by a steady volley of firing.

With deadly effect the machine guns raked the advancing semi-circle of Mongolians. As the foremost line began suddenly to melt away, the rest of the sorcerers wavered and presently came to a halt. They now were not more than a hundred feet from us. At a command, they all dropped down upon the ground, the ones with rifles in front, and began to return our fire.

I had drawn my revolver and joined in the fight—and so had Dr. Gresham beside me. But in our excitement we had remained on our feet, and I now heard the astronomer shouting at me:

"Lie down! *Lie down!*"

Even as I dropped, my hat was knocked off by a bullet; but, unharmed, I stretched out and continued shooting.

Pausing to slip a fresh magazine of cartridges into my automatic, I suddenly became aware that a vast wind was starting to blow out of the east; the very air seemed alive and quivering.

The Chinamen still outnumbered us heavily, and all at once I realized—chiefly from the lessening of our fire—that their rifle attack was beginning to take effect. Glancing about, I saw five or six of the seamen lying motionless.

At this juncture one of the machine guns jammed, and while its crew was trying to fix it the yellow devils took toll of several more of

our men. I now saw that only six of us were
left to fight.

Simultaneously I became half conscious of
a strange, mysterious something going on about
us—a subtle, ghostly change, not on the earth
itself, but in the air above—some throbbing,
indefinable suggestion of impending doom—of
the end of things.

Snatching a glance over my shoulder, I saw
arising upon the eastern horizon a black, monstrous cloud of appalling aspect—a spuming
billow of sable mist—twisting, flying, lifting
into the heavens with tremendous speed. And
each moment the wind was growing more
violent.

Was this, after all, to be the finish? Was
the world—the white man's world, which we
had fought so hard to save—to go to smash
through these yellow devils' fiendishness? Now
that we had come within actual sight of the
machinery that was the cause of it all, was our
task to remain unfinished?

With a terrible cold fury clutching at my
heart, I crawled quickly forward, discharging
my revolver steadily as I went, to lend a hand
with the disabled machine gun.

But as I reached it Ensign Hallock dropped
the weapon, with a gesture of uselessness, and
moved quickly back to the mortars. Out of
the corner of my eye I saw him trying to fire
the things, and a wave of fierce joy seized me.

But the task caused the naval officer to half
raise himself from the ground, and as he did
so I saw him clutch at a bleeding gash on his
head and fall forward; then he lay still.

An instant later the Chinamen leaped to their feet with a loud cry and charged upon us. They, too, were greatly reduced in numbers, but there were only four of us now, so nothing remained but an attempt at retreat. As we did so we began hurling our hand grenades, all the while moving slowly in the only direction we could go—toward the brink of the precipice.

Suddenly, above the crack of the rifles and the exploding of the grenades, an enormous roaring burst forth in the east—a sinister screaming of immeasurable forces, moaning, hooting, shrieking across the world—the weird, awful voice of the wounded planet's stupendous agony.

This new terror attracted so much attention that there was a momentary pause in the sorcerers' onslaught, and in that brief lull I noted that our grenades had wrought terrible havoc among the Chinamen, reducing their number to a mere handful. Dr. Gresham saw this at the same time, and shouted to us to let them have it again with the missiles.

Apparently sensing the purport of this command, the Chinamen sprang forward, seeking to engage us at too close range for the grenades to be used. But several of the missiles met them almost at their first leap, and when the hurricane of shrapnel abated, there remained only three of the yellow fiends to continue the attack.

But at the same time I made the grim discovery that on our side Dr. Gresham and I alone survived!

With the realization that it had now come
to a hand-to-hand encounter, I braced myself
to meet the shock as the trio darted forward.
I somehow felt that nothing mattered any
longer, anyway, for so tremendous had become
the earth-tumult that it seemed impossible the
planet could resist disruption many minutes
more.

Nevertheless, the passions of a wild animal
surged within me; a sort of madness steeled
my muscles.

One powerful, thick-set Chinaman leaped
upon Dr. Gresham and the two went down in
a striking, clawing test of strength. A second
later the remaining pair hurled themselves upon
me.

I whipped out my revolver just as one fellow
seized me from the front, and, pressing the
weapon against his body, I fired. In a moment
he relaxed his hold and crumpled down at my
feet. The other chap now had me around the
neck from the rear and was shutting off my
wind. Round and round we staggered, as I
vainly sought to loosen his hold. Before long
everything went black in front of me and I
thought I was done for—when I heard faintly,
in a daze, the crack of a revolver. Quickly the
grip about my neck fell away.

When I began to come to myself again I
saw Ensign Hallock sitting up on the ground,
his face covered with blood, but wielding the
revolver that had ended the career of my last
adversary.

At the same time I saw that the officer was
trying desperately to train his weapon upon

something behind me. Looking about, I saw Dr. Gresham and his opponent rolling over and over on the ground, almost at the edge of the precipice, struggling frantically for possession of a knife. Because of their rapid changes of position, Hallock dared not shoot, for fear of hitting the scientist.

Just then the Chinaman came on top for an instant, and I leaped forward, aiming my revolver at him. The trigger snapped, but there was no report. The weapon was empty.

Less than a dozen feet now separated me from the wrestlers, when the Celestial suddenly jerked the knife free and raised it for a swift stroke.

With all my strength I hurled the empty revolver at the yellow devil. It struck him squarely between the eyes. The knife dropped and he clutched at his face, at the same time struggling to his feet to meet the new attack.

Freed from the struggle, Dr. Gresham's figure relaxed as in a swoon.

Instantly I was after the Chinaman—without a thought of his bull-like strength. I was seeing red. The furious joy of the primeval man-hunter—the lust for blood—turned my head. My one idea was to kill.

Leaping over the prostrate scientist, I flung myself at the last of the sorcerers. He had retreated three or four feet, and now stood at bay upon the iron bridge that ran along the top of the water mains, overhanging the precipice. As I dashed at him he stepped quickly aside. I missed him—and my heart leaped into my throat as I stumbled across the peri-

lous eyrie and brought up against the outer rail,
which seemed to sway.

I staggered, seized the rod, and saved myself.
Far, far below, jagged rocks and the roof of
the Seuen-H'sin's power house greeted my gaze.

And at the same time—although I was not
conscious of paying attention to it—I became
sensible of the fact that the monstrous cloud
above the horizon was soaring swiftly, beating
its black wings close to the sun—and that a
weird twilight, a ghostly gloom, was settling
over everything. From the distance, too, still
came that appalling uproar.

As I recovered my balance the Chinaman
bounded at me. But his foot caught in the
grating and he stumbled to his knees. Instantly
I threw myself upon him. My knee bored
into the small of his back; my fingers sank
into his throat. *I had him!* If I could keep
my hold a little while the life would be strangled
from his body.

In spite of his disadvantage, the fellow
staggered to his feet. And there above the
void—upon that narrow steel framework, protected only by its leg-high rail—we began a
life-and-death struggle.

I hung on, like a mountain lion upon the
back of its prey, while the Chinaman lurched
and twisted this way and that.

Once he staggered against the railing, lost
his footing, swung around—and I hung out
over empty space, a drop of fully 300 feet.
I thought the end had come—that we would
topple off into the void. But his mighty
strength pulled us back upon the grating—the

whole slight structure seeming to sway and creak as he did so.

I tightened my grip upon his throat, digging my fingers into his windpipe, until I felt the life ebbing out of him in a steady flow. My own strength was almost gone, but the primitive desire to kill kept me clinging there tenaciously.

At last he began to weaken. In his death throes he lurched about in a circle—until his foot slipped through a manhole above one of the ladders, and he fell across the rail with a choking moan. With me hanging upon his back he began to slip outward and downward, inch by inch.

I knew the end had come. He was falling —and I was falling with him. But thoughts of my own death were smothered in a wild rejoicing. I had conquered this yellow fiend! Everything grew blurred before my eyes as we sagged toward the final plunge into the gorge.

Suddenly my ankles were seized in a stout grip, and I felt myself being dragged back from the sickening void. With this, I loosened my hold upon the Chinaman's throat, and his body went hurtling past me to its doom.

Another instant and I was off the rocking bridge, upon solid ground, and Dr. Ferdinand Gresham was shaking me in an effort to restore my senses.

He had recovered from his own fainting spell just in time to save me from being dragged over the cliff.

Swiftly I drew myself together. The weird twilight was deepening. But a few feet away

I beheld Ensign Hallock busy at the mortars and mines, preparing to touch them off.

He motioned to us to run. We did so. In a moment his work was finished and he took after us.

Back along the ridge we fled, away from the danger of the coming blast.

A couple of hundred yards distant and about fifty feet below us, a bare promontory jutted out from the hillside, affording an unobstructed view of the whole region—the crumbling mountains upon the horizon, the power plant at the base of the cliff, and the bare space behind us where the mines were about to end the career of the sorcerers' workshop.

We started to descend to this plateau—when suddenly I dragged my companions back and pointed excitedly below, exclaiming:

"Look! Look!"

There in the center of the promontory, seemingly all alone, stood the arch-fiend of all this havoc—the high priest of the sorcerers, Kwo-Sung-tao!

Apparently the old fellow had chosen this spot whence he could view in safety his followers' attack upon our party. He had not heard my outcry behind him, and remained absorbed in the Titanic upheaval of the distant mountains.

As I looked down upon his shriveled figure, a wave of savage joy swept over me! At last fate was strangely playing into our hands! Quite unsuspecting, the most menacing figure of the ages—the master mind of diabolical achievement, the would-be "dictator of human destiny"—had been cast into our net for final vengeance!

Just then the mortars boomed, and two charges of high explosives went hurtling toward the roof of the power house.

Kwo-Sung-tao wheeled and stared off toward the opposite promontory. Seeing nothing, he hesitated in alarm. He did not look around in our direction.

Another instant and the explosives fell squarely upon the roof of the building, and with two frightful detonations—so close together that they seemed almost as one—the whole structure burst asunder, vanished in a flying tornado of debris. For a few moments nothing was visible save a tremendous geyser of dirt, steel, concrete, and bits of machinery.

While the air was filled with this gust of wreckage, my gaze sped back to the leader of the Seuen-H'sin.

The old man stood still, petrified by this sudden destruction of all his hopes and work. What agony of soul he was enduring in that moment I could only guess. His mummified figure seemed suddenly to have shriveled unbelievably—to be actually withering before our eyes!

Just then the mines under the water mains went off, ripping the conduits to tatters—and the immense hydraulic force, suddenly released, roared down the precipice, tearing the ground at the bottom of the gorge away to the foundation rock and obliterating the last scrap of wreckage!

Almost at the same moment Dr. Gresham
left us and plunged down the slope toward the
high priest, as if to settle the score with him
alone.   Recovering from our surprise, we
followed rapidly.

Apparently sensing the danger, Kwo-Sung-
tao suddenly glanced around. As he beheld
Dr. Gresham he pulled himself together and
I saw a look of malignity come over his face
such as I never before nor since have seen upon
a human countenance!   It was as if he sought
to blast his enemy with a glance!

The demoniacal fury of that gaze actually
caused the astronomer to slacken his rush.

Promptly the old sorcerer's hand darted
beneath his robe and came out with a revolver.
But before the weapon could be aimed I had
snatched a hand grenade and hurled it at the
Chinaman.   The missile flew over him, exploding some feet away; but a bit of its metal must
have hit the old fellow, inflicting a serious
wound, for he dropped the revolver and clutched
at his side.

As he did so he turned his eyes upon me—
and the blood seemed to freeze within my
veins!   Not to my dying day shall I forget the
awful power of that look!

But only for a second did this last—for I
had already drawn another grenade and was
in the act of hurling it.   This time the bomb
fell directly at the feet of the high priest and
burst with deadly force.

Even while the old man's eyes were boring
through me with that unearthly fury, Kwo-
Sung-tao was blown to fragments!

An instant later the sun vanished, and a ghostly semi-night fell like a thunderbolt!

It was several days later when Dr. Ferdinand Gresham, Ensign Hallock and I returned to the Mare Island navy yard at San Francisco. And there, for the first time, we learned that the world remained intact and was out of danger.

When we had ascertained that we three were the only survivors of our expedition, we had started wandering over the mountains through the semi-darkness until we found the destroyer. Unable to navigate the vessel, we had taken the hydroplane, which Hallock knew how to handle, and started south. Engine trouble had prolonged our trip.

Back from the grave, as it seemed, we listened with tremendous elation to the story of the wounded planet's convalescence.

That last terrible upheaval, just before the destruction of the sorcerers' power plant, had seemed for a time to be the actual beginning of the end. But, instead, it had proved to be the climax—after which the earthquakes had begun rapidly to die out. Scientists now declared that before long the earth would regain its normal stability.

With our return, the story of the Seuen-H'sin was given to the public. So universal became the horror with which that sect was regarded that an international expedition proceeded into China and dealt vigorously with the sorcerers.

The tremendous changes that had been wrought in the surface of the planet presently lost their novelty.

And New York and other cities that had been destroyed, or partly destroyed, speedily were rebuilt.

Here I must not omit one other strange incident connected with these events.

One evening, nearly two years after our encounter with the sorcerers, Dr. Gresham and I were sitting at the window of his New York apartment, idly watching the moon rise above the range of housetops to the east of Central Park.

Suddenly I began to stare at the disk with rapt interest. Clutching the astronomer by the sleeve, I exclaimed excitedly:

"Look there! Odd I never noticed it before! The face of the Man in the Moon is the living image of that Chinese devil Kwo-Sung-tao!"

"Yes!" agreed Dr. Greshman with a shudder. "And it makes my flesh creep even to look at it!"

Ooze

By Anthony M. Rud

In the heart of a second-growth piney-woods jungle of southern Alabama, a region sparsely settled save by backwoods blacks and Cajans, stands a strange, enormous ruin.

Interminable trailers of Cherokee rose, white-laden during a single month of spring, have climbed the heights of its three remaining walls. Palmetto fans rise knee-high above the base. A dozen scattered live-oaks, now belying their nomenclature because of choking tufts of gray Spanish moss and two-foot circlets of mistletoe parasite which have stripped bare of foliage the gnarled, knotted limbs, lean fantastic beards against the crumbling brick.

Immediately beyond, where the ground becomes soggier and lower — dropping away hopelessly into the tangle of dogwood, holly, poison-sumac and pitcher-plants that is Moccasin Swamp—undergrowth of ti-ti and anis has formed a protecting wall impenetrable to all save the furtive ones. Some few outcasts utilize the stinking depths of that sinister swamp, distilling "shinny" or "pure cawn" liquor for illicit trade.

I knew "shinny," therefore I did not purchase it for personal consumption. A dozen times I bought a quart or two, merely to establish credit among the Cajans, pouring away the vile stuff immediately into the sodden ground. It seemed then that only through filtration and condensation of their dozens of weird tales regarding "Daid House" could I arrive at understanding of the mystery and weight of horror hanging about the place.

Certain it is that out of all the superstitious cautioning, head-wagging and whispered nonsensities I obtained only two indisputable facts. The first was that no money, and no supporting battery of ten-gage shotguns loaded with chilled shot, could induce either Cajan or darky of the region to approach within five hundred yards of that flowering wall! The second fact I shall dwell upon later.

Perhaps it would be as well, as I am only a mouthpiece in this chronicle, to relate in brief why I came to Alabama on this mission.

I am a scribbler of general fact articles, no fiction writer as was Lee Cranmer. Lee was my roommate during college days. I knew his family well, admiring John Corliss Cranmer even more than I admired the son and friend—and almost as much as Peggy Breede whom Lee married.

Work kept me to the city. Lee, on the other hand, coming of wealthy family—and, from the first, earning from his short-stories and novel royalties more than I wrested from editorial coffers—needed no anchorage. He and Peggy honeymooned a four-month trip to

Alaska, visited Honolulu next winter, fished for salmon on Cain's River, New Brunswick, and enjoyed the outdoors at all seasons.

They kept an apartment in Wilmette, near Chicago, yet, during the few spring and fall seasons they were "home," both preferred to rent a suite at one of the country clubs to which Lee belonged. I suppose they spent thrice five times the amount Lee actually earned, yet for my part I only honored that the two should find such great happiness in life and still accomplish artistic triumph.

They were honest, zestful young Americans, the type—and pretty nearly the *only* type—two million dollars can not spoil. John Cranmer, father of Lee, though as different from his boy as a microscope is different from a painting by Remington, was even farther from being dollar-conscious. He lived in a world bounded only by the widening horizon of biological science—and his love for the two who would carry on the Cranmer name.

Many a time I used to wonder how it could be that so gentle, clean-souled and lovable a gentleman as John Corliss Cranmer could have ventured so far into scientific research without attaining small-caliber atheism. Few do. He believed both in God and in humankind. To accuse him in murdering his boy and the girl wife who had come to be loved as the mother of baby Elsie—as well as blood and flesh of his own family—was a gruesome, terrible absurdity! Yes, even when John Corliss Cranmer was declared unmistakably insane.

Lacking a relative in the world, baby Elsie was given to me—and the middle-aged couple who had accompanied the three as servants through half of the known world. Elsie would be Peggy over again. I worshiped her, knowing that if my stewardship of her interests could make of her a woman of Peggy's loveliness and worth I should not have lived in vain. And at four Elsie stretched out her arms to me after a vain attempt to jerk out the bobbed tail of Lord Dick, my tolerant old Airedale—and called me "papa."

I felt a deepdown choking . . . yes, those strangely long black lashes some day might droop in fun or coquetry, but now baby Elsie held a wistful, trusting seriousness in depths of ultramarine eyes—that same seriousness which only Lee had brought to Peggy.

Responsibility in one instant became double. That she might come to love me as more than foster-parents was my dearest wish. Still, through selfishness I could not rob her of rightful heritage; she must know in after years. And the tale that I would tell her must be the horrible suspicion which had been bandied about in common talk!

I went to Alabama, leaving Elsie in the competent hands of Mrs. Daniels and her husband, who had helped care for her since birth.

In my possession, prior to the trip, were the scant facts known to authorities at the time of John Corliss Cranmer's escape and disappearance. They were incredible enough.

For conducting biological research upon forms of protozoan life, John Corliss Cranmer

had hit upon this region of Alabama. Near
a great swamp teeming with microscopic organ-
isms, and situated in a semi-tropical belt where
freezing weather rarely intruded to harden the
bogs, the spot seemed ideal for his purpose.

Through Mobile he could secure supplies
daily by truck. The isolation suited. With
only an octoroon man to act as chef, houseman and valet for the times he entertained no
visitors, he brought down scientific apparatus,
occupying temporary quarters in the village of
Burdett's Corners while his woods house was
in process of construction.

By all accounts the Lodge, as he termed it,
was a substantial affair of eight or nine rooms,
built of logs and planed lumber bought at Oak
Grove. Lee and Peggy were expected to spend
a portion of each year with him; quail, wild
turkey and deer abounded, which fact made
such a vacation certain to please the pair.

This was in 1907, the year of Lee's marriage.
Six years later, when I came down, no sign of
a house remained except certain mangled and
rotting timbers projecting from viscid soil—
or what seemed like soil. A twelve-foot wall
of brick had been built to enclose the house
completely! One portion had fallen *inward!*

II

I WASTED weeks of time at first, interviewing
officials of the police department at Mobile,
the town marshals and county sheriffs of
Washington and Mobile counties, and officials

of the psychopathic hospital from which Cranmer had made his escape.

In substance the story was one of baseless homicidal mania. Cranmer the elder had been away until late fall, attending two scientific conferences in the North, and then going abroad to compare certain findings with those of a Dr. Gemmler of Prague University. Unfortunately, Gemmler was assassinated by a religious fanatic shortly afterward.

Search of Gemmler's notes and effects revealed nothing save an immense amount of laboratory data on *karyokinesis*—the process of\ chromosome arrangement occurring in first growing cells of higher animal embryos. Apparently Cranmer had hoped to develop some similarities, or point out differences between hereditary factors occurring in lower forms of life and those half-demonstrated in the cat and monkey. The authorities had found nothing that helped me. Cranmer had gone crazy; was that not sufficient explanation? Perhaps it was for them, but not for me—and Elsie.

But to the slim basis of fact I was able to unearth:

No one wondered when a fortnight passed without appearance of any person from the Lodge. Why should any one worry? A provision salesman in Mobile called up twice, but failed to complete a connection. He merely shrugged. The Cranmers had gone away somewhere on a trip. In a week, a month, a year, they would be back. Meanwhile he lost commissions, but what of it? He had no responsibility for these queer nuts up there in the piney-woods. Crazy? Of course! Why should any guy with millions to spend shut himself up among the Cajans and draw microscope-enlarged notebook pictures of what the salesman called "germs?"

A stir was aroused at the end of the fortnight, but the commotion confined itself to building circles. Twenty carloads of building brick, fifty bricklayers, and a quarter-acre of fine-meshed wire—the sort used for screening off pens of rodents and small marsupials in a zoological garden—were ordered, *damn expense, hurry!* by an unshaved, tattered man who identified himself with difficulty as John Corliss Crammer. A certified check for the total amount, given in advance, and another check of absurd size slung toward a labor *entrepreneur,* silenced objection, however. These millionaires were apt to be flighty. When they wanted something they wanted it at tap of the bell. Well, why not drag down the big profits? A poorer man would have been jacked up in a day. Cranmer's fluid gold bathed him in immunity of criticism.

The encircling wall was built, and roofed with netting which drooped about the squat-pitch of the Lodge. Curious inquiries of workmen went unanswered until the final day.

Then Cranmer, a strange, intense apparition more shabby than a quay dereliet, assembled the workmen. In one hand he grasped a wad of blue slips—fifty-six of them. In the other he held a Luger automatic.

"I offer each man a thousand dollars for *silence!*" he announced. "As an alternative—

death! You know little. Will all of you consent to swear upon your honor that nothing which has occurred here will be mentioned elsewhere? By this I mean *absolute* silence! You will not come back here to investigate anything. You will not tell your wives. You will not open your mouths even upon the witness stand in case you are called! My price is one thousand apiece.

"In case one of you betrays me *I give you my word that this man shall die!* I am rich. I can hire men to do murder. Well, what do you say?"

The men glanced apprehensively about. The threatening Luger decided them. To a man they accepted the blue slips—and, save for one witness who lost all sense of fear and morality in drink, none of the fifty-six has broken his pledge, so far as I know. That one bricklayer died later in delirium tremens.

It might have been different had not John Corliss Cranmer escaped.

III

THEY found him the first time, mouthing meaningless phrases concerning an amœba—one of the tiny forms of protoplasmic life he was known to have studied. Also he leaped into a hysteria of self-accusation. He had murdered two innocent people! The tragedy was his crime. He had drowned them in ooze! God!

Unfortunately for all concerned, Cranmer, dazed and indubitably stark insane, chose to perform a strange travesty on fishing four miles to the west of his lodge—on the farther border of Moccasin Swamp. His clothing had been torn to shreds, his hat was gone, and he was coated from head to foot with gluey mire. It was far from strange that the good folk of Shanksville, who never had glimpsed the eccentric millionaire, failed to associate him with Cranmer.

They took him in, searched his pockets—finding no sign save an inordinate sum of money—and then put him under medical care. Two precious weeks elapsed before Dr. Quirk reluctantly acknowledged that he could do nothing more for this patient, and notified the proper authorities.

Then much more time was wasted. Hot April and half of still hotter May passed by before the loose ends were connected. Then it did little good to know that this raving unfortunate was Cranmer, or that the two persons of whom he shouted in disconnected delirium actually had disappeared. Alienists absolved him of responsibility. He was confined in a cell reserved for the violent.

Meanwhile, strange things occurred back at the Lodge—which now, for good and sufficient reason, was becoming known to dwellers of the woods as Dead House. Until one of the walls fell in, however, there had been no chance to see—unless one possessed the temerity to climb either one of the tall live oaks, or mount the barrier itself. No doors or opening of any sort had been placed in that hastily constructed wall!

By the time the western side of the wall fell, not a native for miles around but feared the spot far more than even the bottomless, snake-infested bogs which lay to west and north.

The single statement was all John Corliss Cranmer ever gave to the world. It proved sufficient. An immediate search was instituted. It showed that less than three weeks before the day of initial reckoning, his son and Peggy had come to visit him for the second time that winter—leaving Elsie behind in company of the Daniels pair. They had rented a pair of Gordons for quail hunting, and had gone out. That was the last any one had seen of them.

The backwoods negro who glimpsed them stalking a covey behind their two pointing dogs had known no more—even when sweated through twelve hours of third degree. Certain suspicious circumstances, having to do only with his regular pursuit of "shinny" transportation, had caused him to fall under suspicion at first. He was dropped.

Two days later the scientist himself was apprehended—a gibbering idiot who sloughed his pole, holding on to the baited hook, into a marsh where nothing save moccasins or an errant alligator could have been snared.

His mind was three-quarters dead. Cranmer then was in the state of the dope fiend who rouses to a sitting position to ask seriously how many Bolshevists were killed by Julius Cæsar before he was stabbed by Brutus, or why it was the Roller canaries sang only on Wednesday evenings. He knew that tragedy of the most sinister sort had stalked through his life—but little more, at first.

Later the police obtained that one statement that he had murdered two human beings, but never could means or motive be established. Official guess as to the means was no more than wild conjecture; it mentioned enticing the victims to the noisome depths of Moccasin Swamp, there to let them flounder and sink.

The two were his son and daughter-in-law, Lee and Peggy!

IV

BY FEIGNING coma—then awakening with suddenness to assault three attendants with incredible ferocity and strength—John Corliss Cranmer escaped from Elizabeth Ritter Hospital. How he hid, how he managed to traverse sixty-odd intervening miles and still balk detection, remains a minor mystery to be explained only by the assumption that maniacal cunning sufficed to outwit saner intellects.

Traverse these miles he did, though until I was fortunate enough to uncover evidence to this effect, it was supposed generally that he had made his escape as stowaway on one of the banana boats, or had buried himself in some portion of the nearer woods where he was unknown. The truth ought to be welcome to householders of Shanksville, Burdett's Corners and vicinage—those excusably prudent ones who to this day keep loaded shotguns handy and barricade their doors at nightfall.

The first ten days of my investigation may be touched upon in brief.   I made headquarters in Burdett's Corners, and drove out each morning, carrying lunch and returning for my grits and piney-woods pork or mutton before nightfall. My first plan had been to camp out at the edge of the swamp, for opportunity to enjoy the outdoors comes rarely in my direction.   Yet after one cursory examination of the premises I abandoned the idea.   I did not *want* to camp alone there.   And I am less superstitious than a real estate agent.

It was, perhaps, psychic warning; more probably the queer, faint, salty odor as of fish left to decay, which hung about the ruin, made too unpleasant an impression upon my olfactory sense.   I experienced a distinct chill every time the lengthening shadows caught me near Dead House.

The smell impressed me.   In newspaper reports of the case one ingenious explanation had been worked out.   To the rear of the spot where Dead House had stood—inside the wall —was a swamp, hollow, circular in shape. Only a little real mud lay in the bottom of the bowl-like depression now, but one reporter on the staff of *The Mobile Register* guessed that during the tenancy of the Lodge it had been a fishpool.   Drying up the water had killed the fish, which now permeated the remnant of mud with this foul odor.

The possibility that Cranmer had needed to keep fresh fish at hand for some of his experiments silenced the natural objection that in a country where every stream holds garpike, bass, catfish and many other edible varieties, no one would dream of stocking a stagnant puddle.

After tramping about the enclosure, testing the queerly brittle, desiccated top stratum of earth within and speculating concerning the possible purpose of the wall, I cut off a long limb of chinaberry and probed the mud. One fragment of fish spine would confirm the guess of that imaginative reporter.

I found nothing resembling a piscal skeleton, but established several facts. First, this mud crater had definite bottom only three or four feet below the surface of remaining ooze. Second, the fishy stench became stronger as I stirred. Third, at one time the mud, water, or whatever had comprised the balance of content, had reached the rim of the bowl. The last showed by certain marks plain enough when the crusty, two-inch stratum of upper coating was broken away. It was puzzling.

The nature of that thin, desiccated effluvium which seemed to cover everything even to the lower foot or two of brick, came in for next inspection. It was strange stuff, unlike any earth I ever had seen, though undoubtedly some form of scum drained in from the swamp at the time of river floods or cloudbursts, which in this section are common enough in spring and fall. It crumbled beneath the fingers. When I walked over it, the stuff crumbled hollowly. In fainter degree it possessed the fishy odor also.

I took some samples where it lay thickest upon the ground, and also a few where there seemed to be no more than a depth of a sheet of paper. Later I would have a laboratory analysis made.

Apart from any possible bearing the stuff might have upon the disappearance of my three friends, I felt the tug of article interest—that wonder over anything strange or seemingly inexplicable which lends the hunt for fact a certain glamor and romance all its own. To myself I was going to have to explain sooner or later just why this layer covered the entire space within the walls and was not perceptible *anywhere* outside! The enigma could wait, however—or so I decided.

Far more interesting were the traces of violence apparent on wall and what once had been a house. The latter seemed to have been ripped from its foundations by a giant hand, crushed out of semblance to a dwelling, and then cast in fragments about the base of wall —mainly on the south side, where heaps of twisted, broken timbers lay in profusion. On the opposite side there had been such heaps once, but now only charred sticks, coated with that gray-black, omnipresent coat of desiccation, remained. These piles of charcoal had been sifted and examined most carefully by the authorities, as one theory had been advanced that Cranmer had burned the bodies of his victims. Yet no sign whatever of human remains was discovered.

The fire, however, pointed out one odd fact which controverted the reconstructions made by detectives months before. The latter, suggesting that the dried scum had drained in from the

swamp, believed that the house timbers had
floated out to the sides of the wall—there to
arrange themselves in a series of piles! The
absurdity of such a theory showed even more
plainly in the fact that *if* the scum had filtered
through in such a flood, the timbers most certainly had been dragged into piles *previously!*
Some had burned—*and the scum coated their
charred surfaces!*

What had been the force which had torn
the Lodge to bits as if in spiteful fury? Why
had the parts of the wreckage been burned,
the rest to escape?

Right here I felt was the keynote to the
mystery, yet I could imagine no explanation.
That John Corliss Cranmer himself—physically
sound, yet a man who for decades had led a
sedentary life—could have accomplished such
destruction, unaided, was difficult to believe.

V

I TURNED my attention to the wall, hoping for
evidence which might suggest another theory.

That wall had been an example of the worst
snide construction. Though little more than
a year old, the parts left standing showed
evidence that they had begun to decay on the day
the last brick was laid. The mortar had fallen
from the interstices. Here and there a brick
had cracked and dropped out. Fibrils of the
climbing vines had penetrated crevices, working
for early destruction.

And one side already had fallen.

It was here that the first glimmering suspicion of the terrible truth was forced upon me. The scattered bricks, even those which had rolled inward toward the gaping foundation lodge, *had not been coated with scum!* This was curious, yet it could be explained by surmise that the flood itself had undermined this weakest portion of the wall. I cleared away a mass of brick from the spot on which the structure had stood; to my surprise I found it exceptionally firm! Hard red clay lay beneath! The flood conception was faulty; only some great force, exerted from inside or outside, could have wreaked such destruction.

When careful measurement, analysis and deduction convinced me—mainly from the fact that the lowermost layers of brick all had fallen *outward,* while the upper portions toppled *in*— I began to link up this mysterious and horrific force with the one which had rent the Lodge asunder. It looked as though a typhoon or gigantic centrifuge had needed elbow room in ripping down the wooden structure.

But I got nowhere with the theory, though in ordinary affairs I am called a man of too great imaginative tendencies. No less than three editors have cautioned me on this point. Perhaps it was the narrowing influence of great personal sympathy—yes, and love. I make no excuses, though beyond a dim understanding that some terrific, implacable force must have made this spot his playground, I ended my ninth day of note-taking and investigation almost as much in the dark as I had been while a thousand miles away in Chicago.

Then I started among the darkies and Cajans.
A whole day I listened to yarns of the days
which preceded Cranmer's escape from Elizabeth Ritter Hospital—days in which furtive
men sniffed poisoned air for miles around Dead
House, finding the odor intolerable. Days in
which it seemed none possessed nerve enough
to approach close. Days when the most fanci-
ful tales of mediæval superstitions were spun.
These tales I shall not give; the truth is incredible enough.

At noon upon the eleventh day I chanced
upon Rori Pailleron, a Cajan—and one of the
least prepossessing of all with whom I had
come in contact. "Chanced" perhaps is a bad
word. I had listed every dweller of the woods
within a five-mile radius. Rori was sixteenth
on my list. I went to him only after interviewing all four of the Crabiers and two whole
families of Pichons. And Rori regarded me
with the utmost suspicion until I made him a
present of the two quarts of "shinny" purchased of the Pichons.

Because long practise has perfected me in
the technique of seeming to drink another man's
awful liquor—no, I'm not an absolute pro-
hibitionist; fine wine or twelve-year-in-cask
Bourbon whisky arouses my definite interest—
I fooled Pailleron from the start. I shall omit
preliminaries, and leap to the first admission
from him that he knew more concerning Dead
House and its former inmates than any of the
other darkies or Cajans roundabout.

"...But I ain't talkin'. *Sacré!* If I should
open my gab, what might fly out? It is for

keeping silent, y'r damn' right! . . ."

I agreed. He was a wise man—educated to some extent in the queer schools and churches maintained exclusively by Cajans in the depths of the woods, yet naive withal.

We drank. And I never had to ask another leading question. The liquor made him want to interest me; and the only extraordinary topic in this whole neck of the woods was the Dead House.

Three-quarters of a pint of acrid, nauseous fluid, and he hinted darkly. A pint, and he told me something I scarcely could believe. Another half-pint . . . But I shall give his confession in condensed form.

He had known Joe Sibley, the octoroon chef, houseman and valet who served Cranmer. Through Joe, Rori had furnished certain indispensables in the way of food to the Cranmer household. At first, these salable articles had been exclusively vegetable—white and yellow turnip, sweet potatoes, corn and beans—but later, *meat!*

Yes, meat especially—whole lambs, slaughtered and quartered, the coarsest variety of piney-woods pork and beef, all in immense quantity!

IV

IN DECEMBER of the fatal winter, Lee and his wife stopped down at the Lodge for ten days or thereabouts.

They were en route to Cuba at the time,

intending to be away five or six weeks.   Their
original plan had been only to wait over a day
or so in the piney-woods, but something caused
an amendment to the scheme.

The two dallied. Lee seemed to have become
vastly absorbed in something—so much absorbed that it was only when Peggy insisted
upon continuing their trip, that he could tear
himself away.

It was during those ten days that he began
buying meat. Meager bits of it at first—a
rabbit, a pair of squirrels, or perhaps a few
quail beyond the number he and Peggy shot.
Rori furnished the game, thinking nothing of
it except that Lee paid double prices—and
insisted upon keeping the purchases secret from
other members of the household.

"I'm putting it across on the Governor,
Rori!" he said once with a wink. "Going to
give him the shock of his life. So you mustn't
let on, even to Joe, about what I want you to do.
Maybe it won't work out, but if it does!. .
Dad'll have the scientific world at his feet!
He doesn't blow his own horn anywhere near
enough, you know."

Rori didn't know. He hadn't a suspicion what
Lee was talking about.   Still, if this rich young
idiot wanted to pay him a half-dollar in good
silver coin for a quail that any one—himself
included—could knock down with a five-cent
shell, Rori was well satisfied to keep his mouth
shut. Each evening he brought some of the
small game.   And each day Lee Cranmer
seemed to have use for an additional quail or
so . . .

When he was ready to leave for Cuba, Lee came forward with the strangest of propositions. He fairly whispered his vehemence and desire for secrecy! He would tell Rori, and would pay the Cajan five hundred dollars—half in advance, and half at the end of five weeks when Lee himself would return from Cuba—provided Rori agreed to adhere absolutely to a certain secret program. The money was more than a fortune to Rori; it was undreamt-of affluence. The Cajan acceded.

"He wuz tellin' me then how the ol' man had raised some kind of pet," Rori confided, "an' wanted to get shet of it. So he give it to Lee, tellin' him to kill it, but Lee was sot on foolin' him. W'at I ask yer is, w'at kind of pet is it w'at lives down in a mud sink *an' eats a couple hawgs every night?*"

I couldn't imagine, so I pressed him for further details. Here at last was something which sounded like a clue.

He really knew too little. The agreement with Lee provided that if Rori carried out the provisions exactly, he should be paid extra and at his exorbitant scale of all additional outlay, when Lee returned.

The young man gave him a daily schedule which Rori showed. Each evening he was to procure, slaughter and cut up a definite—and growing—amount of meat. Every item was checked, and I saw that the items ran from five pounds up to *forty!*

"What, in heaven's name, did you do with it?" I demanded, excited now and pouring him

an additional drink for fear caution might
return to him.

"Took it through the bushes in back an' slung
it in the mud sink there! An' suthin' come up
an' drug it down!"

"A 'gator?"

"*Diable!* How should I know? It was dark.
I wouldn't go close." He shuddered, and the
fingers which lifted his glass shook as with
sudden chill. "Mebbe you'd of done it, huh?
Not *me,* though! The young fellah tole me to
sling it in, an' I slung it.

"A couple times I come around in the light,
but there wasn't nuthin' there you could see.
Jes' mud, an' some water. Mebbe the thing
didn't come out in daytimes . . ."

"Perhaps not," I agreed, straining every
mental resource to imagine what Lee's sinister
pet could have been. "But you said something
about *two hogs a day?* What did you mean
by that? This paper, proof enough that you're
telling the truth so far, states that on the
thirty-fifth day you were to throw forty pounds
of meat—any kind—into the sink. Two hogs,
even the piney-woods variety, weigh a lot more
than forty pounds!"

From this point onward, Rori's tale became
more and more enmeshed in the vagaries
induced by bad liquor. His tongue thickened.
I shall give his story without attempt to
reproduce further verbal barbarities, or the
occasional prodding I had to give in order to
keep him from maundering into foolish jargon.

Lee had paid munificently. His only objection to the manner in which Rori had carried

out his orders was that the orders themselves
had been deficient. The pet, he said, had grown
enormously. It was hungry, ravenous. Lee
himself had supplemented the fare with huge
pails of scraps from the kitchen.

From that day Lee purchased from Rori
whole sheep and hogs! The Cajan continued
to bring the carcasses at nightfall, but no longer
did Lee permit him to approach the pool. The
young man appeared chronically excited now.
He had a tremendous secret—one the extent
of which even his father did not guess, and
one which would astonish the world! Only a
week or two more and he would spring it.
First he would have to arrange certain data.

Then came the day when everyone disappeared from Dead House. Rori came around
several times, but concluded that all of the
occupants had folded tents and departed—
doubtless taking their mysterious "pet" along.
Only when he saw from a distance Joe, the
octoroon servant, returning along the road on
foot toward the Lodge, did his slow mental
processes begin to ferment. That afternoon
Rori visited the strange place for the next to
last time.

He did not go to the Lodge itself—and there
were reasons. While still some hundreds of
yards away from the place a terrible, sustained
screaming reached his ears! It was faint, yet
unmistakably the voice of Joe! Throwing a
pair of number two shells into the breach of his
shotgun, Rori hurried on, taking his usual path
through the brush at the back.

He saw—and as he told me even "shinny"

drunkenness tied his chattering tones—Joe, the octoroon. Aye, he stood in the yard, far from the pool into which Rori had thrown the carcasses—*and Joe could not move!*

Rori failed to explain in full, but *something*, a slimy, amorphous something, which glistened in the sunlight, already had engulfed the man to his shoulders! Breath was cut off. Joe's contorted face writhed with horror and beginning suffocation. One hand—all that was free of the rest of him—beat feebly upon the rubbery, translucent thing that was engulfing his body!

Then Joe sank from sight . . .

VII

FIVE days of liquored indulgence passed before Rori, alone in his shaky cabin, convinced himself that he had seen a fantasy born of alcohol. He came back the last time—to find a high wall of brick surrounding the Lodge, including the mud-pool into which he had thrown the meat!

While he hesitated, circling the place without discovering an opening—which he would not have dared to use, even had he found it—a crashing, tearing of timbers, and persistent sounds of awesome destructions came from within. He swung himself into one of the oaks near the wall. And he was just in time to see the last supporting stanchions of the Lodge give way *outward!*

The whole structure came apart. The roof fell in—yet seemed to move after it had fallen!

Logs of wall deserted layers of plywood in the
grasp of the shearing machine!

That was all. Suddenly intoxicated now,
Rori mumbled more phrases, giving me the
idea that on another day when he became sober
once more, he might add to his statements, but
I—numbed to the soul—scarcely cared. If
that which he related was true, what nightmare
of madness must have been consummated here!

I could vision some things now which concerned Lee and Peggy, horrible things. Only
remembrance of Elsie kept me faced forward
in the search—for now it seemed almost that
the handiwork of a madman must be preferred
to what Rori claimed to have seen! What had
been the sinister, translucent thing? That
glistening thing which lumped upward about a
man, smothering, engulfing?

Queerly enough, though such theory as came
most easily to mind now would have outraged
reason in me if suggested concerning total
strangers, I asked myself only what details of
Rori's revelation had been exaggerated by fright
and fumes of liquor. And as I sat on the
creaking bench in his cabin, staring unseeing
as he lurched down to the floor, fumbling with
a lock box of green tin which lay under his
cot, and muttering, the answer to all my questions lay within reach!

It was not until next day, however, that I
made the discovery. Heavy of heart I had
re-examined the spot where the Lodge had
stood, then made my way to the Cajan's cabin
again, seeking sober confirmation of what he
had told me during intoxication.

In imagining that such a spree for Rori would be ended by a single night, however, I was mistaken. He lay sprawled almost as I had left him. Only two factors were changed. No "shinny" was left—and lying open, with its miscellaneous contents strewed about, was the tin box. Rori somehow had managed to open it with the tiny key still clutched in his hand.

Concern for his safety alone was what made me notice the box. It was a receptacle for small fishing-tackle of the sort carried here and there by any sportsman. Tangles of Dowagiac minnows, spoon-hooks ranging in size to silver-backed number eights, three reels still carrying line of different weights, spinners, casting-plugs, wobblers, floating baits, were spilled out upon the rough plank flooring where they might snag Rori badly if he rolled. I gathered them, to save him an accident.

With the miscellaneous assortment in my hands, however, I stopped dead. Something had caught my eye—something lying flush with the bottom of the lock box! I stared, and then swiftly tossed the hooks and other impedimenta upon the table. What I had glimpsed there in the box was a looseleaf notebook of the sort used for recording laboratory data! And Rori scarcely could read, let alone *write!*

Feverishly, a riot of recognition, surmise, hope and fear bubbling in my brain, I grabbed the book and threw it open. At once I knew that this was the end. The pages were scribbled in pencil, but the handwriting was that precise chirography I knew as belonging to John Corliss Cranmer, the scientist!

" . . . Could he not have obeyed my instructions! Oh, God! This . . . "

These were the words at top of the first page which met my eye.

Because knowledge of the circumstances, the relation of which I pried out of the reluctant Rori only some days later when I had him in Mobile as a police witness for the sake of my friend's vindication, is necessary to understanding, I shall interpolate.

Rori had not told me everything. On his late visit to the vicinage of Dead House he saw more. A crouching figure, seated Turk-fashion on top of the wall, appeared to be writing industriously. Rori recognized the man as Cranmer, yet did not hail him. He had no opportunity.

Just as the Cajan came near, Cranmer rose, thrust the notebook, which had rested across his knees, into the box. Then he turned, and tossed outside the wall both the locked box and a ribbon to which was attached the key.

Then his arms raised toward heaven. For five seconds he seemed to invoke the mercy of Power beyond all of man's scientific prying. And finally he leaped, *inside!* . . .

Rori did not climb to investigate. He knew that directly below this portion of wall lay the mud sink into which he had thrown the chunks of meat!

VIII

THIS is a true transcription of the statement I inscribed, telling the sequence of actual events at Dead House. The original of the statement now lies in the archives of the detective department.

Cranmer's notebook, though written in a precise hand, yet betrayed the man's insanity by incoherence and frequent repetitions. My statement has been accepted now, both by alienists and by detectives who had entertained different theories in respect to the case. It quashes the noisome hints and suspicions regarding three of the finest Americans who ever lived—and also one queer supposition dealing with supposed criminal tendencies in poor Joe.

John Corliss Cranmer went insane for sufficient cause!

As readers of popular fiction know well, Lee Cranmer's forte was the writing of what is called, among fellows in the craft, the pseudo-scientific story. In plain words, this means a yarn, based upon solid fact in the field of astronomy, chemistry, anthropology or whatnot, which carries to logical conclusion unproved theories of men who devote their lives to searching out further nadirs of fact.

In certain fashion these men are allies of science. Often they visualize something which has not been imagined even by the best of men from whom they secure data, thus opening new horizons of possibility. In a large way Jules Verne was one of these men in his day; Lee Cranmer bade fair to carry on the work in worthy fashion—work taken up for a period by an Englishman named Wells, but abandoned for stories of a different, and in my humble opinion a less absorbing type.

Lee wrote three novels, all published, which dealt with such subjects—two of the three secured from his own father's labors, and the other speculating upon the discovery and possible uses of interatomic energy. Upon John Corliss Cranmer's return from Prague that fatal winter, the father informed Lee that a greater subject than any with which the young man had dealt now could be tapped.

Cranmer, senior, had devised a way in which the limiting factors in protozoic life and growth could be nullified; in time, and with co-operation of biologists who specialized upon *karyokinesis* and embryology of higher forms, he hoped—to put the theory in pragmatic terms —to be able to grow swine the size of elephants, quail or woodcock with breasts from which a hundredweight of white meat could be cut away, and steers whose dehorned heads might butt at the third story of a skyscraper!

Such result would revolutionize the methods of food supply, of course. It also would hold out hope for all undersized specimens of humanity—provided only that if factors inhibiting growth could be deleted, some method of stopping gianthood also could be developed.

Cranmer the elder, through use of an undescribed (in the notebook) growth medium of which one constituent was *agar-agar,* and the use of radium emanations, had succeeded in bringing about apparently unrestricted growth in the paramœcium protozoan, in certain of the vegetable growths (among which were bacteria), and in the amorphous cell of protoplasm known as the amœba—the last a single cell

containing only nucleolus, nucleus, and a space
known as the contractile vacuole which somehow aided in throwing off particles impossible
to assimilate directly. This point may be
remembered in respect to the piles of lumber
left near the outside walls surrounding Dead
House!

When Lee Cranmer and his wife came south
to visit, John Corliss Cranmer showed his son
an amœba—normally an organism visible under
low-power microscope—which he had absolved
from natural growth inhibitions. This amœba,
a rubbery, amorphous mass of protoplasm, was
the size then of a large beef liver. It could
have been held in two cupped hands, placed
side by side.

"How large could it grow?" asked Lee, wide-
eyed and interested.

"So far as I know," answered the father,
"there is *no* limit—now! It might, if it got
food enough, grow to be as big as the Masonic
Temple!

"But take it out and kill it. Destroy the
organism utterly—burning the fragments—else
there is no telling what might happen. The
amœba, as I have explained, reproduces by
simple division. Any fragment remaining might
be dangerous."

Lee took the rubbery, translucent giant cell
—but he did not obey orders. Instead of
destroying it as his father had directed, Lee
thought out a plan. Suppose he would grow
this organism to tremendous size? Suppose,
when the tale of his father's accomplishment
were spread, an amœba of many tons weight

could be shown in evidence? Lee, of somewhat sensational cast of mind, determined instantly to keep secret the fact that he was not
destroying the organism, but encouraging its
further growth.   Thought of possible peril
never crossed his mind.

He arranged to have the thing fed—allow-
ing for normal increase of size in an abnormal
thing.   It fooled him only in growing much
more rapidly.   When he came back from Cuba
the amœba practically filled the whole of the
mud sink.   He had to give it much greater
supplies. . . .

The giant cell came to absorb as much as
two hogs in a single day.   During daylight,
while hunger still was appeased, it never
emerged, however. That remained for the time
that it could secure no more food near at hand
to satisfy its ravenous and increasing appetite.

Only instinct for the sensational kept Lee
from telling Peggy, his wife, all about the
matter.   Lee hoped to spring a coup which
would immortalize his father, and surprise his
wife terrifically.   Therefore, he kept his own
counsel—and made bargains with the Cajan,
Rori, who supplied food daily for the shapeless
monster of the pool.

The tragedy itself came suddenly and unex-
pectedly.   Peggy, feeding the two Gordon
setters that Lee and she used for quail hunting,
was in the Lodge yard before sunset.   She
romped alone, as Lee himself was dressing.

Of a sudden her screams cut the still air!
Without her knowledge, ten-foot pseudopods—
those flowing tentacles of protoplasm sent forth

by the sinister occupant of the pool—slid out and around her putteed ankles.

For a moment she did not understand. Then, at first suspicion of the horrid truth, her cries rent the air. Lee, at that time struggling to lace a pair of high shoes, straightened, paled, and grabbed a revolver as he dashed out.

In another room a scientist, absorbed in his notetaking, glanced up, frowned, and then— recognized the voice, shed his white gown and came out. He was too late to do aught but gasp with horror.

In the yard Peggy was half engulfed in a squamous, rubbery something which at. first glance he could not analyze.

Lee, his boy, was fighting with the sticky folds, and slowly, surely, losing his own grip upon the earth!

IX

John Corliss Cranmer was by no means a coward. He stared, cried aloud, then ran indoors, seizing a shotgun and a hunting-knife. The knife was ten inches long and razor-keen.

Cranmer rushed out again. He saw an indecent fluid something—which as yet he had not had time to classify—lumping itself into a six-foot-high center before his very eyes! It looked like one of the micro-organisms he had studied! One grown to frightful dimensions. An amœba!

There, suffocated in the rubbery folds, yet still apparent beneath the glistening ooze of this monster, were two bodies. They were dead. Nevertheless he attacked the flowing senseless monster with his knife. Shot would do no good. And he found that even the deep slashes made by his knife closed together and healed. The monster was invulnerable to ordinary attack!

A pair of pseudopods sought out his ankles, attempting to bring him low. Both of these he severed—and escaped. Why did he try? He did not know. The two whom he had sought to rescue were dead, buried under folds of this horrid thing he knew to be his own discovery and fabrication. Then it was that revulsion and insanity came upon him.

There ended the story of John Corliss Cranmer, save for one hastily scribbled paragraph —evidently written at the time Rori had seen him atop the wall.

May we not supply with assurance the intervening steps?

Cranmer was known to have purchased a whole pen of hogs, a day or two following the tragedy. These animals never were seen again. During the time the wall was being constructed is it not reasonable to assume that he fed the giant organism within—to keep it quiet? His scientist brain must have visualized clearly the havoc and horror which could be wrought by the loathsome thing if it ever were driven by hunger to flow away from the Lodge and prey upon the countryside!

With the wall once in place, he evidently figured that starvation or some other means which he could supply would kill the thing.

One of the means had been made by setting fire to several piles of the disgorged timbers; probably this had no effect whatever.

The amœba was to accomplish still more destruction. In the throes of hunger it threw its gigantic, formless strength against the house walls *from the inside;* then every edible morsel within was assimilated, the logs, rafters and other fragments being worked out through the contractile vacuole.

During some of its last struggles, undoubtedly, the side wall of brick was weakened—not to collapse, however, until the giant amœba no longer could take advantage of the breach.

In final death lassitude, the amœba stretched itself out in a thin layer over the ground. There it succumbed, though there is no means of estimating how long a time intervened.

The last paragraph in Cranmer's notebook, scrawled so badly that it is possible some words I have not deciphered correctly, read as follows:

"In my work I have found the means of creating a monster. The unnatural thing, in turn, has destroyed my work and those whom I held dear. It is in vain that I assure myself of innocence of spirit. Mine is the crime of presumption. Now, as expiation—worthless though that may be—I give myself——"

It is better not to think of that last leap, and the struggle of an insane man in the grip of the dying monster.

www.ingramcontent.com/pod-product-compliance
Lightning Source LLC
Chambersburg PA
CBHW05074925O626
47155CB00005B/1994